Nyifie Brothers Publishing

VAMPIRES IN THE WHITE CITY

THE VAMPIRE MAURICE (A FAT VAMPIRE SIDE SERIES) - BOOK 3

JOHNNY B. TRUANT

ONE

MONSTER

DR. RICE LOOKED at the clock, knowing the vampire would arrive for his appointment exactly on time, exactly at the top of the hour. There were now just two minutes left, and after a bit of centering she felt as prepared for this little experiment as she was going to get. Instead of sitting in her usual chair, she sat behind her desk. Instead of holding a notepad, she held only a pen. She'd marshaled all her concentration. She wanted to get focused now, then *stay* focused after he arrived. As their session began, she intended to remain as single-minded as this little meditation could make her — something she'd had trouble doing in the past thanks to the nagging voice inside her.

She watched the progress of the clock's second hand. She tried to imagine time slowing, then stopping. Some-times, when she focused very hard on *now* instead of *future* or *past*, the alien voice inside — the one that sounded a lot like her lisping husband — would fall quiet. She'd had a theory for several days now (spawned not long after Maurice's last visit, actually) that if she could summon that timeless state while in the vampire's presence, something important would happen. Or *could* happen. Or, if she was very still, something might be *allowed* to happen. But usually that's not how it was. Usually, the second voice was present at all times during her appointments with Maurice. Not in a controlling way and not in an all-seeing way, but just ... *nudging* her. Affecting her questions and her behavior. It was like the will of an overprotective parent lingering even after the child has become an adult, influencing their behaviors and habits.

Still, Annabel wondered why it felt so important to shut up her own nagging presence — even if only for the first few seconds of Maurice's visit. *Why* was it so important to shove that lisping voice away and have a few seconds alone with the vampire?

Answer: It *wasn't* important.

Answer: Annabel was pretty sure she was crazy to obsess over it at all. She kept getting the feeling that the presence inside *knew* she was trying to shut it out and was amused in the same way a dog's owner is amused when it chases its tail. Who was she trying to fool? *You can't hide from your own eyes. You can't shrink back from your own intuition* ... if that's what this was.

The doorknob turned. Annabel's meditative state broke instantly. Despite trying to hold her mind quiet, it grew noisy as soon as the vampire entered. The internal voice of her husband seemed to laugh with amusement.

It must have looked strange, because Maurice stopped in the doorway to stare at her.

"Am I interrupting something?"

"No," she said, embarrassed.

You've had your fun, that internal voice seemed to add. *Now do ath you're told.*

But she felt (and probably seemed) like she'd been

caught masturbating. She was still behind her desk, eyes wide and unsure where to focus, not quite willing to look him in the face. She felt her cheeks redden. The voice inside was laughing, enjoying her discomfort.

You can't hide, it said. *Why would you think you could hide?*

But another presence inside — this one new and never heard-from before — seemed to stand up in response. If Maurice had been describing it in his vampire way, he might have called this second one *the force of blood.* Whereas her husband's internal voice made Annabel reticent, this one made her feel strong. Whereas the first voice cowed her, the sense of blood empowered her.

Then it was gone. The sense of her husband's voice was gone, too.

And all awareness — of the internal voices, of intuition, of her husband's manipulations, even of her own efforts to focus with Maurice because something unexplored was still vital between them — was gone.

And with that, she was just a therapist again. She had no thought other than helping her patient.

Maurice unfroze. Still watching her, he moved to the couch. Then he seemed to decide that what had felt wrong actually wasn't (Annabel certainly didn't feel anything amiss ... *now*), and together they sighed into what had become their usual routine.

Maurice on his back, taking in the detail of the ceiling.

Annabel moving to her usual soft chair, pad on knee, legs crossed right over left.

A moment of pregnant silence.

Then:

"I'm supposed to talk first," Maurice said. "Right?"

"However you'd like," Annabel replied.

"But last time, you gave me shit for not saying anything after I arrived. So really it's *not* 'however I'd like.' I *am* supposed to talk first."

"It really is up to you, Maurice."

The clock ticked. Traffic was an unsteady whisper beyond the windows.

"You know," Maurice said, "I think these sessions help me. I wouldn't come back if I didn't think they were helping. But they also kind of suck."

"How so?"

"I've started to question things I've always taken for granted."

"Like what?"

"Like myself. My very identity. I've always looked the same, right? Well, this morning I looked in the mirror and thought, 'Maurice, *you've always looked the same.*'"

"All right."

Maurice turned his head, apparently unimpressed that she was unimpressed. "Well, *humans* don't always look the same! You look a little different every day. I can *make* myself look different, but only by changing my clothes, changing my hair, stuff like that. *You* constantly evolve. Vampires like me are unchanging."

"And that bothers you?"

"I guess it'd be more accurate to say 'it *occurs* to me.' Doesn't it bother you to work with someone whose very nature prohibits change?"

"I think that even a vampire," Annabel said, "is capable of change in the ways that matter."

Maurice was shaking his head, lost in thought. Therapy could do this to people, Annabel knew. It could make the confusion worse before it got better.

"You know, historically the world has thought of us as

monsters," he said. "I was looking in the mirror this morning, seeing this person who doesn't change, who doesn't age, who will never evolve into something different or more. And I thought, 'Maybe I *am* a monster.'"

"That's hardly fair," Annabel said. "You are what you are."

"I don't even mean it in a bad way. I mean it as objective fact. Maybe I'm a ... a *thing*."

"You are vampire. I am human. *Those* are objective facts. 'Monster' isn't objective. That term carries judgment, like good or bad, right or wrong. You're not a monster unless you choose to be, Maurice."

He chewed his lip. Fortunately for Maurice, his fangs weren't down as he did it. "So it's defined by deeds, you mean?"

"Something like that."

"But I've killed. I've killed so many."

"Ever killed an innocent?"

Maurice didn't think about that, but he didn't answer right away, either. She realized they hadn't just stumbled across this line of discussion. He'd *led* them here, a problem already on his shoulders.

"Maurice?" she prompted, wanting an answer to the question.

"Not exactly. Maybe. I don't know."

"How can you not know something like that?"

"It's complicated."

When he didn't volunteer more, she brought up something she recalled from his last session — or, perhaps, something the voice inside had *made sure* she recalled.

She flipped through her notes, then found one of the few things Maurice had said last visit that she'd written down verbatim.

"Last time you were here, you said, 'I went to the Fair, did my thing, met a monster, then returned most of a year later.' What did you mean by *that* mention of 'monster'?"

"The Fair ..." he said.

"In fact, you told me to ask you about the Fair this visit. And about Holmes."

Now he squinted. "I mentioned Holmes?"

Annabel flipped through her notes. Of course he had. Only ... maybe he hadn't. Maybe someone she'd spoken to on the phone *after* the appointment had offered that name to go with Maurice's mention of the 1893 Chicago World's Fair. Who would that have been? She remembered it but also didn't remember it at all. She'd felt that way a lot this month — as if she was recalling a dream, or chronically hypnotized.

She knew it was a slip, and rushed to cover.

Decisively, she said, "Yes."

"I don't remember mentioning him by name." Then he spoke into the unseen distance. "And to think. All this talk of monsters."

"This isn't helping me understand, Maurice."

He stood. He went to the window, his back to her. She recognized the body language, same as might come from a human. Seeing that same language from Maurice made her shiver. Vampires weren't supposed to get spooked. They weren't supposed to get chills. They weren't supposed to act like they'd seen — or perhaps met — ghosts.

"What else did I tell you?" he asked.

"About the Fair?"

"That and other things, yes."

"You said that your on-again, off-again friend Raphael Michaud sent you. That you decided, together, that you should go." As she spoke, she remembered more and more.

She spoke confidently, no longer needing to lie. "Paris had just had their big exposition. They'd unveiled the Eiffel Tower. Then Chicago threatened to top Paris with its own expo, and you wanted to go 'as a representative of European pride.'" She knew more, of course, but there would be time for that later. She'd done some online research about the Chicago World Fair between their last session and this one. She'd researched Holmes, too, though she'd keep that to herself for now.

"Yes," he said, nodding to himself. He moved away from the window and back to the couch. He sat, then laid back in his trademark position. "Yes, it makes sense to start there. With my trip to America — my *real* first trip, this time."

"Whenever you're ready," Annabel said.

Then her mind — and the second mind inside her — stilled itself to listen.

TWO

THE GOOD DOCTOR

THE PROPRIETOR WAS TALL, well-built, and handsome with beautiful blue eyes. At first I thought he might be a vampire. He was so charming, I'd probably have felt glamoured if I didn't know I couldn't be.

We were in the reception room of his hotel — a second-floor chamber on one of the building's front corners. In the other front corner was a waiting room, to which I'd been led first by a nondescript man who'd introduced himself as Benjamin Pitezel. Apparently you waited, *then* were received. Both rooms, I imagined, would be bright and sunny during daytime, with bay windows that protruded over 63rd Street in twin semicircles.

The way up had disoriented me, and not just because of the evening dim. The first floor housed a pharmacy, a barber, and some shops including a tinsmith. We'd ascended a staircase that led upward south of the windows I was now looking through, and had needed to wind past and through rooms to get to the hotel's front. The floorplan was odd, from what I'd seen so far: rooms where there should be hallways, hallways where there should be rooms. The corridors were too narrow and I couldn't shake the feeling that the proportions were all wrong: outer walls too far in, as if they were overly thick or there were hidden chambers behind the brick. But then again, I'd heard weird things about this place before arriving. It was half the reason I'd come — to this hotel specifically..

"Mr. Toussaint?"

I turned to find the good doctor himself, as Pitezel had promised.

Before I could answer, he amended his question: "Or should I perhaps say, *'Monsieur* Toussaint'?"

I didn't want to smile. My guard was up, and frankly all of America had disgusted me so far. I'd heard disturbing things as well as weird things — among them, how easy it was for people to disappear in the hurly-burly of Chicago, never to be seen again. People were regularly dismembered or decapitated by rail cars — enough that everyone seemed to know someone who'd lost parts. The city was filthy. The lake seemed ready to catch on fire. The air was acrid, full of smoke and spent fuel. Carriages rattled by with little concern for who they rolled over, and there was horseshit absolutely everywhere.

But I smiled anyway. His manner was intoxicating.

The doctor went on. "Benjamin tells me you are from France. *C'est beau, n'est-ce pas?*"

"Are you referring to Chicago, or France?"

"France, of course. Chicago is home, but I will not delude myself as to its absent splendor."

"You've been to France?" I elongated the "a" in "France" from the nasal "eh" sound to the more fluid "aah," my accent lulled deeper by the doctor's cordial way.

"But of course. Mr. Toussant. Please. Have a seat."

I sat. I found myself saying, "Call me Maurice."

We exchanged introductions and pleasantries, including his flawless recitation of several bits of French literature, proving his culture. I kept smiling, though that's not my usual way — not now, not back then. Especially not so soon after leaving my erstwhile business partner, Raphael. Back in April of 1893, when I'd met the good doctor, I'd been kind of a dick. Not too proud to admit it, either.

But I was softening under this charming man's soft blue gaze.

"So. How can I help you, Maurice?"

"Simple enough. I have come for the fair. I would like to have a room."

He gave a pacifying smile. "Alas, I do not have lodging to offer. We are at capacity."

I'd seen this coming. Still, I wanted to ask why Pitezel had lead me upstairs only to be rejected. I didn't know why this place had called me to its front door, but it had. Just like the owner seemed unable to send me away — again, for reasons unknown. It'd be trite to say I'd come to 63rd and Wallace for a reason, but that's exactly how it felt. I'd get a room here … or claw their eyes out trying.

My eyebrows raised. I'd prepared a lie for just this occasion.

"I understood that my reservation was already in hand," I said.

"How so, sir?"

"By mail." I flashed an envelope I'd placed in my jacket pocket — nothing to do with a reservation at all. I put the envelope back before he could see what it was. "May I speak with Emeline Cigrande? She should have my name already down."

Also a lie. I'd known they might be full, just as I'd

known I meant to get a room regardless. So I'd asked around about the hotel — which locals called "the castle" — before entering. I learned the desk had been managed by a woman named Emeline, now departed. For some reason, the people I'd asked clammed up when I asked for details, but it didn't matter; I had what I needed. All that mattered was that if I really *had* sent mail in advance of my visit, it'd be Emeline I'd have corresponded with.

The doctor met my eyes. The way people on the street had avoided the topic, I half expected him to flinch as if there were a secret to hide. An affair, perhaps — the one man I'd glamoured had already divulged that rumor.

"Ms. Cigrande has since moved away," he said.

"Well then. You must still have my reservation in your reservation book."

"Forgive me. We have had problems with staff. Any reservations she may or may not have taken before leaving have gone missing."

"But surely you would not refuse my stay after I've come all this way on good faith, with expectations of lodging?"

"Apologies," he said. "I can recommend many other boarding houses in the city if you would like."

I *wouldn't* like. No other hotel or boarding house would do. I didn't know why, but an unshakable blood hunch compelled me to stay here. The hunch was like a needle in my brain, steering me to this place — and this place alone.

I made myself imperious. It was easy; Americans expected it from us.

I slapped my hand on the coffee table. "Unacceptable. I wish to be close enough to the fair to be able to attend any day I like without requiring transportation, yet I want to be far enough from it to avoid the crowds. I did my part, sir, corresponding with your staff via letter and telegram. *This* is where I booked my reservation, and *this* is where I intend to stay." I lowered my tone, becoming more reasonable. "Surely you keep a room or two available for special guests. Surely you are not *truly* at capacity. How can such a large building fill completely, and yet I have seen no one in the hallways?"

I waited for an answer. I knew some rooms were empty; I'd asked the locals about comings and goings. At most the hotel had five boarders — nowhere near the number of rentable rooms. So why was he refusing?

The doctor's eyes narrowed. His politeness slipped a notch, now that he saw I wasn't leaving.

"You would not like it here," he said. "I had problems with the architect. The floorplan is practically a maze."

More lies. I knew he'd been his own architect.

"I do not mind. I enjoy mazes."

"It is dark."

"I see so many gas lamps," I countered. "It must be very bright once they are turned on."

"Many of the lamps are ... are disconnected," Pitezel said with a glance at the doctor. There was meaning there, as if problems with gas lines were something they'd fought about.

"Then I will carry a lantern."

My host looked at his assistant, then leaned forward. He addressed me with elbows on his knees.

"May I be honest?"

"Of course."

"This hotel specializes in lodging for women. Many would feel ... *threatened* ... by a strange man in their midst."

"Oh? But I know men have stayed here."

"Locals. Friends. Those were men I've known personally."

"Whereas I ...?"

"You're a stranger from a foreign land. And what's more, you are applying after dark. It may frighten those unaccustomed to such things. Apologies again, sir. I do not wish to offend, but ..." He spread his arms as if to say, ... *but what can you do?*

My curiosity deepened. I met his eyes, knowing I meant to stay here, willing to persuade my way into a room in any way I could. Two things stopped me from glamouring him there and then. The first was Pitezel, who'd see me do it. The second, however, prickled my skin. Not everyone can be glamoured. Some are immune, and I knew the man before me was one of those. Beneath his soft gaze was an internal hardness — a deep will that would not be bent. Glamour is like hypnosis. You can fight it if you know what's coming. You can turn your mind off, if your mind is unusual or overly strong. Or (and this is how the doctor struck me) if the mind in question is broken.

I sat up. I stood. Defeated despite my best efforts, for now.

"Well then. I suppose that's all there is to it," I said.

"I'm very sorry."

"Perhaps I will try again, once the town has gotten to know me."

"Perhaps."

There were footsteps behind us — a pattering sort of tread, sloppy and urgent. A few seconds later, a small man appeared. He was less than four feet tall, dressed in elaborate showman's clothes, wearing his hat indoors like a cretin. He had a naked face, either unable to grow a mustache or unwilling.

"Shit, fuck," said the dwarf. He came right at me, ignoring the others. Only once he was close enough to grab my hand — which he did — did he look to the doctor and Pitezel before returning his attention to me.

"Holy fuck, Maurice!" he blurted. "You won't fucking believe this. You *have* to come outside. There's something you've gotta fucking see!"

I didn't know what to say. I had no idea who the man was and hadn't heard "fuck" four times in one speech ever before. The other men seemed offended by everything about him: his brusque manner, his profanity, his refusal to doff his bowler indoors. He even smelled a little: the must of horse hair, as if he worked in a stable.

"Fucking sorry," the dwarf told my hosts.

They mumbled, unsure how to respond.

I met his eyes. Without words, I tried to ask, *Who are you?*

Instead of answering — with words or without — he took my arm and tugged.

"You okay, man? Look. You've gotta come with me. There's some crazy, crazy shit out here!"

"Please," said the doctor. "Language. There are ladies lodging here."

"You mean you two?" the dwarf asked. "Fuck that. Let's go, Maurice. No time to waste."

"What do you want to show me ..." I paused, feeling the other men's wondering stare, feeling a hunch to play along with the new man's game. He was wearing a name, sewn onto the breast of his jacket. "... 'Ferris,'" I read.

It was like he'd bit into a lemon. "Come on," he said, dragging me harder from the hotel. "Chop fucking chop."

THREE
FREAKS

"Jesus Christ," said the dwarf once our heels hit the gas-lit sidewalk along 63rd Street. "Jesus fucking Christ, Maurice."

"Religious man, are you?"

"Did you seriously call me 'Ferris' in there?"

"It's the name on your jacket."

"It's the name of the *wheel*," he said. "One of my many jobs is helping put up the *Ferris fuckin' wheel*, you dickbag."

I looked east. Yes, the infamous *Ferris wheel*. Of all the absurd things said in Europe about the upcoming Chicago Fair, boasts about the Wheel made Raphael and I laugh the hardest. Did the Americans really think they could build such a monstrous contraption without massive fatalities? Did they think it wouldn't collapse under its own weight, killing the thousands of passengers it was supposed to be able to carry at once? I'd seen the plans; Raphael's coercion and blackmail network had pulled some strings. On paper, the thing looked like a toy grown enormous. Its circles and spokes were tiny things, thin as spun silk. It was a joke — or would be, if they ever managed to finish it.

Looking now, I could see its support members poking into space like rotten teeth. There was no finished wheel yet, and opening day was right around the corner.

"*You* are on the construction crew?" I asked.

"What's that supposed to mean? You think I can't do it because I'm small? I'll fuck you up, Maurice. I'll punch you right in the balls!"

"How do you know my name?"

He shrugged. "We knew you were in town."

Too many questions. I didn't know where to start. Who was "we"? How did they know I was in town? Why did they care, what did they want, and how did they know where to find me? Was this small man really on a crew tasked with lifting girders and climbing scaffold? And most pressingly:

"What did you want to show me?" I asked. He'd let go of my arm now that we were outside, but where I'd expected some big presentation, I saw nothing. Then I had it. "Wait. You're part of the freak show, aren't you?"

He hauled back, wound up, and punched me squarely in the testicles. I went down. Vampire or not, getting hit in the nuts hurts. I heal, but I feel pain just fine.

"Fuck your mother!" the dwarf yelled as I squirmed on the street. "What, just because I look different, I must be part of the freak show?"

"Are you?"

"Well ... yeah. But that's just because 1893 isn't a very enlightened time. Society is balls, man. You just wait. A hundred, hundred and fifty years from now, guys like me will be considered special. We'll be all woke."

"Do you mean 'woken'?"

"*Woke!*"

I shrugged. The idea was absurd.

I got to my feet. "You still haven't told me what you

wanted me to see. *Is* it the freak show? Because I've gotta tell you, that's not really my thing."

"Dick," he said. "Even 'different' people need to eat, you know."

I didn't respond. It wasn't clear if my new friend was more offended that I'd assumed he was in the freak show or more concerned about the freak show's success. It was contradictory to hold both views, but he seemed to be holding them just fine.

"There *is* nothing to see. I just needed to get you away from that dickwipe." We walked, me following him somewhere unknown. "My name's Wyatt, by the way. Hardee-fucking-har-har; I know, like Wyatt Fucking Earp, but if you ask me about the gunfight at the OK Corral, I'll separate your balls from your body."

"What is it with you and testicles?"

"Easy reach. If I were taller, I'd grab for your neck scrotum."

"What's a neck scrotum?"

"Shut up, Maurice. You talk too much."

I walked half a block in silence, Wyatt two steps ahead.

"Where are we going?"

"Away from Castle Douchebag."

"What's that?"

"Holmes's hotel." He pointed back at the building we'd left. "That's what we call it."

"Who's 'we'?"

"The freaks."

"The freaks?" I asked.

"FUCK YOU THAT'S OUR WORD AND YOU CAN'T CALL US THAT!"

I closed my mouth.

"Yeah," Wyatt said a few steps later. *"The freaks."*

"How do you know my name?"

"All the freaks know your name. We all know you're here. Even heard about your plans to stay at Castle Skin Sack."

That was ridiculous. Until I was within a mile of the castle, I hadn't *had* plans to stay there. The urge had hit me like bricks less than a half hour ago, building from an itch I'd felt the entire train ride here. By the time I got close, I knew I needed to visit, knew the hotel might refuse, knew I needed stories like the one about Emeline Cigrande to have a chance. The idea that unknown freaks were two steps ahead of even me was too insane to tackle. For right now, anyway.

"'Castle Skin Sack'? I thought it was 'Castle Douchebag'?"

"It's a lot of things." Wyatt spat. "You don't want to stay there, man. Bad news. You think the owner's name is Doctor H. H. Holmes? What a crock. His name is Mudgett. Herman Webster Mudgett. Now he's HHH. Triple H. What kind of a freak names himself Triple H?"

I shrugged.

"I overheard some lady call him by his real name once, and Holmes didn't even care because the only folks heard 'im were us freaks. But that lady? Nobody ever saw her again."

"Maybe she left town."

"Sure. She *left town*. Just like that woman Julia who worked there and her daughter. Just like the front desk girl who replaced her. Just like half the people who check into Butt Palace and never check out."

"Are you implying foul play?"

Wyatt mocked me, repeating my question with a sarcastic lilt. "*Yes, I'm implying foul play.* You wanna talk about *us* being freaks? *That* guy's a freak. He only rents to women."

"He mentioned that."

"Rents to them, then fucks them."

"Um …"

"And then they vanish. It's a thing. We've got connections, us freaks. We're the underbelly of the whole fuckin' fair, baby. *We hear all.*" He pointed at his ears, staring me in the eye to make sure I understood and was duly impressed.

"And?"

"And that guy, Holmes, he makes the ladies cream their petticoats. Not *all* the ladies, though. Not freak ladies, who see right through his bullshit to the creeper beneath. Like Tatiana, our ink lady? She's like, fuck that guy. Not that he doesn't try. The fair's not even open yet and he's always on the midway, stopping by to chat us up. You believe that?"

"Maybe he's a patron of the arts."

"He's a patron of getting a boner when looking at the bearded lady. Or wolf girl. Do you know how many times he's asked to sit on the four-legged woman's lap? I know what he's thinking. He thinks two sets of legs might equal two vaginas. That's not how it works, though. I know." He winked knowingly. "I'm telling you, that guy's off his rocker. Takes a freak to know a freak."

I waited. For a guy who resented my assumption that he was in the freak show, he sure talked about the freak show a lot. For a guy so offended by the word "freak," he sure said it often.

Wyatt went on.

"He's had that building for a few years now, right? Just finished construction of the third floor, but he's been using it for a while. I know some guys who did construction for it. They'd work a few weeks at most, and then Holmes would fire them. Nobody knows the plans for that freak-fucking-show place of his. Nobody knows how all the walls fit together or what he's had installed where. *Nobody*, 'cept Holmes. But man .. everyone loves him. Total charmer. Uses that charm to get whatever he wants. But he's got more missing chicks around him than a farmer with a coyote problem, and nobody sees through that asshole other than us."

"Why don't you go to the police?"

"Who'd listen to a bunch of freaks? Cybil, our lobster girl? She was arrested for having two fingers. FOR HAVING TWO FINGERS WHAT THE FUCK." Wyatt shook his head. "Anyway. You don't want to stay there. You don't want to hang out with that walking taint, or be anywhere near him."

"I can take care of myself," I said.

"What, because you're a vampire? That don't make no difference, asshole."

I stopped. "What did you say?"

"That it don't make no difference."

"I mean the other thing."

"What else did I say?" He scratched his head. "Did I say you were ugly?"

"You said I was ..." But I couldn't repeat it. I wouldn't. Not in America, with all their chaos and lawlessness.

"Oh. Right. I just said that bein' a vampire was no excuse to take risks like that."

"What's a vampire?"

"Oh, fuck you, Maurice."

"And how do you know my name?"

"Bitch, please. I told you. We know it all."

"I'm not a vampire."

"Yes you are."

"Vampires don't exist."

"Do they not exist, or do you not know what they are?"

"Both."

Wyatt laughed at me and kept walking. "Whatever, man."

There was a long quiet between us. Then I said, "I'm serious."

"Look," Wyatt said. "Deny all you want, but I know you're a vampire just like I know your name is Maurice."

I sidestepped the obvious questions and asked another. "What makes you so sure I'm a vampire?"

"Two reasons," Wyatt said. "The first is that after you got into town, we started following you. I saw you trip just outside the station, then get your legs cut off by that streetcar."

I felt myself blush. That had been a total tourist move, getting dismembered by a streetcar.

"The second is that we've got one at the freak show," Wyatt said.

"You've got a vampire at the freak show?"

"What did I tell you about using that word?" he snapped. Then he said, "But yeah. We've got one. He's the reason we knew you were coming, but he'd already made plans tonight to get his fangs sucked. You know."

I didn't know. I didn't want to ask, either.

I looked ahead. The naked posts that might one day support the Ferris Wheel aberration were larger now, as we walked toward the waterfront.

"Where are we going?"

"To the midway."

"To meet your 'vampire'?" I tried to laugh as if I found the word and concept absurd, but the laugh came out flat — more like a mumble. Truth was, Wyatt had me lapped. He knew a lot — and not just about me, either. He knew the city, the fair, the creepy proprietor of the funhouse hotel. He knew my name, my day of arrival, probably why I'd come. That wasn't good news. But with the revelation that the midway freak show included a vampire, at least I was starting to understand the whys and hows of the situation.

"Yeah," Wyatt said. "To meet the vampire."

But I was beginning to suspect I didn't need to *meet* the vampire to know him. I knew him already. We weren't related, but someone in my family line had met him and had a full set of impressions. That relative of mine — no idea who or when or where; it was blood with no head on it — already had a body of knowledge about this one.

Starting with the fact that the freak show vampire's name was—

FOUR

CLOWN

"Eugene?"

The vampire had his back to me. He was wearing some sort of long black garment. From the rear, he appeared to have oiled black hair. We were the same kind of creature, sure. But after reviewing my relative's memories of him during the remainder of the walk, I knew we were nothing alike.

When vampire turned, it was like being punched with a clown. Not *by* a clown, but *with* one — as in, this guy in front of me was clearly kidding ... with his outfit, with his manner, with his way of speaking, with pretty much everything. The kind of kidding that happened when someone used a full-sized clown as a bludgeon.

His lip wrinkled when I used his name. "Don't call me that," he said.

But with Wyatt gone elsewhere and the two of us alone, I found it hard to keep my expression neutral. Despite the sincerity of his request, I kept wanting to laugh in his face.

He stood, then paced the room dramatically. I watched, increasingly amused.

The long black garment turned out to be a cloak, which he wore in grand fashion. It had an upturned collar tall enough to reach the bottoms of his earlobes. He wore a tuxedo shirt, white vest, white bowtie beneath. At his neck hung an ornate six-pointed broach, strung on a colored lanyard like a congressional medal. His black hair was indeed oiled — oiled like a fryer accident. He had it straight back, plastered to his head, a fake little widow's peak inked in the center with a grease pencil. His skin was white, powdered that way, and his lips were painted bright red. He had severe black eyebrows, also inked.

Fighting not to giggle, I said, "Well, then, what *should* I call you?"

"I prefer 'Dracula.'"

"That's not a thing," I said. "Just like that chicken suit isn't a thing."

Dracula bolted forward, suddenly in my face. "The hell it's not," he said. "You think you're so smart? I've met your relatives. We've shared blood. When we have, I've poked around the thoughts that you aren't careful enough to hide. I know all about you, *Maurice Toussant*. You think you can just come to America and piss on the Chicago fair? The fair is *mine*, old man! You're out of touch. Me? *I'm* on the cutting edge. While you were crossing the ocean in a box of dirt, I've been walking the fairgrounds, learning about the future. The other day, I met motherfucking *Tesla*, and that's even before the fair opens its doors. What I'm wearing isn't a chicken suit. It's the *future*."

I looked him over. He pranced, using the cape like a peacock's feathers.

"Okay, then," I said.

"What, you don't believe me? You shouldn't have left Paris. There's a book coming out in a few years by a guy named Bram Stoker that's going to sweep the world. If you'd been paying attention, you would have seen it. There are still years before publication but that book is *already* hot. You just watch. This look?" He flourished for me again. "I *invented* it. They start doing stage performances of Stoker's book, this is how the vampires will dress. Don't mock what's clearly ahead of its time."

"Sure thing, Eugene," I said.

"Dracula," he corrected.

I was already tired of Dracula. Wyatt had taken me through the gate, down the midway, and into the semi-permanent half-tent the freak show called home. It was fascinating. All these unusual people just walking around off-duty, being themselves, going about their business with an acre of hair on their faces or ink over most of their bodies or nails through their skin. I saw the girl with too many legs (but apparently just one vagina, according to Wyatt), the acrobat with no legs, two men conjoined at the waist, and a pair of bald twins with distended skulls that gave me the creeps. No wonder the vampire had joined their ranks. Freaks only came out at night.

I walked away from Dracula's private chambers, back into the main room.

"What?" he said, following. "You think you're too good for me?"

Close. Actually, I didn't care about him.

"Get back here, Maurice!" he called as he pranced after me. "I want to talk to you. *I'm* the reason the freaks knew you were in Chicago. *I'm* the one who told Wyatt where to find you."

"But you didn't come yourself? Now who's 'too good'?"

"Hey. I had ladies to service. Guys too; I don't discriminate. I don't even need to glamour them. They just line up.

You want to know what the best thing is about being a freak show vampire?"

I didn't turn around. I was looking for Wyatt, or possibly the exit.

"It's that I can just *be a vampire*," Dracula went on. "I don't have to hide. The show's got lobster boy and poultry girl and elephant-feet-lady, so why not a vampire? That's how they bill me: *Dracula the Vampire*. I get on stage once a night — three or four times a night, once the fair starts — and I raise my cape like this and hold it over my face like this—" He demonstrated. With his cape over his face, it looked like he was peering over a fence. "—and I go like this." He made eerie, ominous sounds. "Then I tell them I want to suck their blood. And at the end I'll be like, 'Seriously. *I want to suck your blood.*' Every time without fail, two or three people take me up on it, lining up with exposed necks. All the free blood I could ever want! Look, man—" Chasing me now, trying to get me to care. "*Look.* I don't need this gig. But there's blood friggin' *everywhere* here and it'd be a shame not to take advantage. And do you want to know the best part? If you accidentally kill someone: Oh well, it's Chicago and shit happens. Not to mention that the freak girls are ..."

He waited for me to fill the blank, as if I might be in on this joke with him.

"They're *freaks*, man!" he said when I didn't oblige. "Tatiana, the painted lady? She's got a tattoo of my dick on her *neck*. Check it out. It looks like an eggplant, but I'm telling you, it's Steamship Dracula."

The freak show, as I continued walking away from the vampire, was bigger than I'd thought. I couldn't find the exit. I just kept finding more and more performers in more and more rooms. They must have been used to a general lack of privacy. Nobody looked at me and Dracula as we played follow-the-leader through the place.

"You're not impressed," Dracula said. "I get it. Whatever. To each his own. But you've gotta slow down. I'm getting winded here."

That made me stop. I turned to face him.

"You're *winded.*"

Hand on heart, he huffed and puffed. "Just give me a minute."

"You're a supernatural being capable of moving faster than human eyes can see ... and you're *winded.*"

"Are you body-shaming me right now?"

I turned away. Dracula resumed his pursuit.

"All right, all right. I'm not an athlete. That doesn't mean you shouldn't listen to what I have to say."

I stopped again. "Okay. Fine. Bring it. I'm really eager to hear what you have to say. Because as you said, I *did* come here to shit on this fair — or at least scope it out, maybe cause a few problems. I got off my train, snooped around, glamoured some folks, and listened every bit as closely as your man Wyatt thinks the people here listen. I'm no slouch. I already know what I want to do. I heard weird buzz about that hotel on 63rd, and I was all set to get a room. That means I was doing just fine before I met your illustrious self. Now that I've been dragged all the way here ... no, I'm not *impressed.* But that's not even the question, is it? I don't need to be impressed *or* not impressed. I didn't ask for anyone's help, let alone you butting in. So if you want to convince me of something, convince me why I should care. You obviously called me for a reason, and you're posturing for a reason, and now that it's clear I don't give a shit, you're *chasing* me for a reason. So: Out with it. Tell me why I'm here, or I won't be anymore."

Dracula looked like he might challenge that just to save face, but instead he went through a half-dozen expressions ranging from anger to resignation before finally speaking.

"Fine," he said. "But I can't just tell you. I have to show you."

FIVE

BLOOD PERSUASION

WHAT HE HAD to show me, of course, was the exact same hotel I'd just come from. I'd just walked three miles with Wyatt only to turn around and walk those same three miles with Wyatt again, this time joined by what looked like a guy in a Halloween costume. I was pissed. If Dracula wanted to meet me at Holmes's hotel, why hadn't he just come himself the first time?

None of this occurred to Dracula, who seemed concerned only with his own timeline and clearly had his own agenda. When I asked, he just said, "This is definitely more convenient for me." He didn't want to hear how he'd wasted my time. Instead, he wanted to talk about how H. H. Holmes — proprietor of the hotel I'd now twice visited — was evil incarnate.

"He might suck," I mumbled. "'Evil incarnate' is a bit much."

"Hey! Did you grow up here?" Dracula snapped. "Are you from Chicago? There's a lot of bad juju in this town, and I've been here long enough to see my share. I've never really wondered if evil lived here. That felt like a given. It just took me a while to figure out where it was."

I looked over. He couldn't be serious, could he? He was a vampire. If he wanted to see evil, all he had to do was look in a mirror.

Instead, he kept blabbing.

"This city is rotten, Maurice. Before I was turned, I was a newsboy in this city. Do you know how often people tried to catch me and play with my balls?"

"Again with the balls."

"*A lot,*" Dracula went on. He made motions in the air, indicating the streets around us. "This area? I called it 'the molestation zone.' You had to go super fast through here or you'd get molested. It was just a thing that happened, like firecrackers in Chinatown. After a while, I didn't even think it was strange. Just really, *really* inconvenient. It'd be like, man, I got stuff to do. Know what I'm sayin'?"

"Sure?"

"I was fast. My friends were fast. Nobody ever caught us, but they sure tried. Gangs of perverts would chase us with beckoning hands, offering candy. So I know *bad*. I've got a pretty high tolerance for badness in Chicago. But that dude?" He pointed at the hotel, now just across the street. A few gaslights were burning in windows, along with flickering illumination I took to be lanterns. "That dude is creepy on top of creepy."

"Creepy doesn't make him evil," I said.

Dracula didn't reply. When I looked over, he had a hand on his forehead, wincing as if he had a headache. Not because of what I'd said, but because of something else.

"You okay?" Wyatt asked. "Is it ... ?"

"I'm fine."

"You don't *look* fine."

"Let's just get this over with," Dracula said.

"Get *what* over with?" I asked. "Fighting demons?"

Dracula's pained expression immediately cleared. "You just watch," he snapped. "I'm always ahead of the curve. I'm on top of trends like nobody's business. Give it time and everyone will agree with what I'm saying. They'll write books about that guy—" He pointed again at the hotel. "—and call him the devil."

I rolled my eyes but didn't bother to respond. Seemingly satisfied that he'd at least made his case, Dracula started picking his teeth with a thumbnail. Wyatt and I looked at each other. I think he was considering me as a vampire, wondering if the sideshow had gotten a raw deal with its bloodsucker and should consider switching to someone more cosmopolitan.

"Fine," I said, ignoring Wyatt's gaze in favor of Dracula. "What's any of this got to do with me?"

"You've got to get in there. Rent yourself a hotel room."

I practically groaned. "That's exactly what I *was* doing when Wyatt burst in on us."

"Oh yeah? And how was it going?"

There was a long pause. Finally, seeing myself snared, I said, "Holmes refused to rent to me."

"But that couldn't have been a problem for a talented vampire like you, right? You could just glamour him."

I firmed my lips. I knew he'd been snooping through whatever illicit blood-swap he'd done with one of my relatives. Worse, I knew the point he was leading me toward was correct. I didn't like capitulating to Dracula, but I'd come here for a reason I didn't fully understand, and no longer thought it was just to infiltrate the fair. That had always been a nebulous mission anyway. What was I planning to do — bring the Ferris wheel down after it was finished? Burn the Midway Plaisance? Knock the Statue of the Republic into the Great Basin in the Court of Honor? Raphael and I had never planned that far, nor would we have. Paris had had its expo and Chicago's would turn out to be grander. That was a fact by now, and no pissed-off French vampire would honestly be able (or care enough) to stop it. So why *had* I come to Chicago ... really?

"You couldn't glamour Holmes, could you?" Dracula said.

I crossed my arms. Wyatt looked up at both of us, curious where this was headed.

"You know why you couldn't do it, Maurice? It's because he's a dichrome."

"That's ridiculous."

Wyatt said, "What's a dichrome?"

I answered, mostly to rob Dracula of a chance to show off. "A dichrome is a very rare type of human with a schism in their personality. Have you read *The Curious Case of Dr. Jeckyll and Mr. Hyde?*"

"Yes," said Dracula, who I hadn't asked.

"I can't read," said Wyatt, "but I know the gist."

"Dichromes are like that. Two-faced." I looked up at the hotel, which lit as it was reminded me of a face with eyes. "They show one side of themselves to the world and keep another part secret." Today, a psychiatrist might diagnose schizophrenia or multiple personality disorder, but from what I understand it's a mixture of both. In reality it's diagnosed only by supernaturals, seeing as it can't be understood without believing in magic.

"And?" Wyatt asked.

"And to clown-man's point," I said, referring to Dracula, "dichromes are impossible to glamour because only one of those personalities comes out at a time. While you're trying to glamour one part of them, the other keeps trying to wake it back up."

"Well," Dracula said, "they're not *impossible* to glamour. It just takes two vampires to do it — one for each half of their mind."

Finally, I was beginning to understand. Two halves of Holmes to glamour, two vampires in attendance. I was less than interested. Still, I looked up at the building. Dracula, for all his absurdity, wasn't wrong about Holmes. He *had* struck me as strange; he *had* proven hard to glamour; I *had* felt a sense of profound wrongness in his presence. It was like Holmes knew what I was, knew what I wanted, and was able to stop me without effort. Intellectually, I knew I was a million times stronger than Holmes and could end him any time I wanted. But somehow, still, I wondered if I'd be able. Somehow, still, I was just a little bit afraid of him.

"I'll help you get a room," Dracula said, "if you help me."

"I don't need your help. I'll just glamour his partner. Benjamin."

"I've tried to glamour Pitezel," Dracula said. "It's easy, but somehow Holmes always knows. If Holmes were a vampire, I'd say Pitezel was his familiar. In truth, they're both human. But ... well ... I don't know if you've ever met a dichrome before."

I considered saying no, but the truth was I was at a disadvantage. Dracula knew far more about this than I did. It was as plain as the nose two feet below, on Wyatt's face.

"I haven't met one," I admitted.

"Rumor says that if you try to kill one, you have to kill them twice."

And I thought I'd gotten a chill before. I hid it. I didn't like Dracula steering this conversation.

"Somewhere else, then," I said. "It's a big city. I can find other lodging."

"With the fair opening in a week? No way. The city is packed!"

"I'll manage," I told him. "I can be very persuasive."

"Uh-huh. Then tell me: Why did you come here?"

"To investigate the Chicago Fair."

"I meant *here*." He pointed to the sidewalk beneath our feet. "Why, when you got off the train, did you come *here*, to this particular hotel?"

"I just followed my feet."

"Your feet? Or a feeling?"

This was maddening. It was as if I'd written a journal of my travels, and Dracula had read it. This wasn't all coming from blood. I'd have felt him in my mind if he'd stolen this many thoughts. His grasp of my motives meant he was intuitive, or had done research, or was smarter than he looked. Which, to be fair, was pretty easy to do.

"Fine. Thinking back, I was probably following a feeling all along."

"A feeling about this hotel?"

"Once I got close enough and felt its presence, yes." I stared him down. "But how could you know that?"

"Because it's *my* feeling," Dracula explained. "I've been sowing blood into any vampire who'd let me for six months, just trying to get my feelings out to someone who'd listen."

"You *what?*"

I wanted to hit him. If what he'd said was true, it explained our connection but was grossly immoral. We couldn't communicate directly, but if he'd been swapping blood with other vampires, it'd make him some sort of blood hub, all right. But it was disgusting. Swapping blood, other than between lovers, was ... well ... *really gross* in vampire circles.

"I've been broadcasting my feelings about H. H. Holmes forever," he went on. "Nobody I've swapped with has been willing to help, though, and nobody outside the circle picked up on it. So either there aren't many other vampires around, or they're just not reachable through blood ties."

"Maybe they're just ignoring you," I said. It was possible. Dracula was the kind of vampire you crossed the street to keep from admitting you knew.

"But then I felt *you*, all the way across the Atlantic. One of my swap-friends' makers had a French maker. Maybe he and your maker are related."

I doubted it. My maker turned me before Jesus was born.

"I couldn't read your thoughts without partaking of your blood, of course, but I could feel your intention through the ties I'd already made. When you got on that ship from France, I figured this was my one opportunity to reach someone old enough and strong enough to do something about Holmes. I knew you were headed to Chicago before you boarded your train in New York. The bond got stronger and stronger as you came closer, so I started to spend more time thinking about this place — about the big three-story building on 63rd and Wallace. Your coming here was no accident. You were feeling the itching that's been in *my* gut since December."

"What happened in December?"

"A woman named Emeline Cigrande disappeared."

I fought a blink. I didn't want him to know I'd heard the name. I'd even heard about the disappearance. Hell — not two hours earlier, I'd given that name to Holmes himself.

I affected nonchalance. *"And?"*

"She was one of my regular feeders. I ..."

I finally understood. "You didn't just drink her blood. You also got attached to her."

He looked caught. But yes, that was it.

"So *that's* the reason you started acting and dressing like you do," I said. "Trauma."

Dracula's face changed in an instant. He said, "What the hell, man? Are you making fun of me?"

"Oh, without question."

Dracula put his hands on his hips. "Look. I've got a problem and you've got a problem."

"You have a problem," I corrected. *"I'm* all good."

"I need to know what happened to Emeline. For that, I need Holmes ... and to deal with Holmes, I need you."

"He won't just tell you what happened to her, you know," I said. "Even if I help. That's not how dichromes work. Even twice-glamoured, the two halves protect each other."

"I don't need him to *say* anything," Dracula told me. "I just need him to let you stay at his place so that you can investigate. I'm talking about you helping me with good old-fashioned detective work, not brain games."

"Me? How about *you?"*

His hand went toward his head again as if minding a headache. He stopped it short.

"People know me," he said. "I'm a celebrity around here. How can I possibly snoop around if people believe I'm a vampire, or if they keep demanding autographs?"

I stared at the building. I didn't want to do Dracula's bidding on principle. I definitely didn't want to admit the strength of the intuition I'd felt drawing me to this place. Most of all, I didn't want to tell Dracula that his blood hunch had only *primed* my curiosity, not created it. Now that I knew he'd been in my head, I'd closed it off. What remained were my own feelings ... and like Dracula, now that I'd met Holmes, I'd gotten a sticky, couldn't-just-walk-away feeling from the man, too.

"What's in it for me?" I asked.

"Satisfaction," Dracula answered. "The knowledge that you helped right a wrong."

I stared him in the eyes.

"Not enough for you, huh? Fine. Wyatt?"

The dwarf waited for instructions.

"Show him."

Wyatt reached into an inside pocket and removed a small vial the size of the top joint of a pinky finger. Inside was a thick red liquid.

"What's that?" I asked.

And Dracula said, "Answers."

SIX

MACHT

Annabel looked up. "'Answers'? Does that mean it was blood in the vial?"

"Vampire blood," Maurice replied. "Dracula had found the blood of a vampire who'd known things I very much wanted to know. If I sampled the blood Dracula offered me, I'd know those things, too."

"Why not just ask the guy?"

"Because he died. Because he was staked."

That felt ominous to Annabel, but she pushed on.

"What things did you want to know?"

Maurice shifted on the couch. After three sessions, Annabel had gotten a feel for his patterns. Say the wrong thing and he'd clam up. Say a different wrong thing and he'd do what he was doing right now: slithering as his body betrayed discomfort between his ears. She didn't pry. It was more fruitful to wait.

"What have I told you about Celeste?" he asked.

"She's your wife," Annabel answered. "She's around a thousand years old."

"Did I tell you about her turning?"

"Only that you did it. You made her like you made Daisy and Reginald. For all three, you turned them to save their lives."

"But I didn't tell you how it happened with Celeste. I didn't tell you why."

The second presence in Annabel's brain — the part that watched, listened, and came when called — perked up.

Maurice pondered for a long time. Finally he said, "My wife is a strong woman, Dr. Rice. She seems sweet and domestic, and often she is. But there are times she's been anything but sweet. Plenty of times when I've been the weaker one, and Celeste has saved me. Times she's defended our home. By modern standards, a thousand years is still very old for vampires — especially here in America, where the oldest have just a few centuries behind them. Because Celeste has the strength of a thousand years, she doesn't like to talk about what she feels are weaknesses. But I'm not just her maker; I'm also her mate. She can't hide much from me, and when she does, I know it.

"There is only one thing, in all our years together, that she's never let me see. To my internal eye, that thing is a locked black cargo trunk that sits in a corner of her mind. Sometimes it rattles, as if a hideous thing is trapped and trying to escape. I've seen how that box of secrets affects her — how when it rattles, Celeste becomes timid. I know that in the dim, when nobody is watching, something escapes that trunk and prowls the hallways of her mind. I've woken to her screaming, but by the time I delve into blood, whatever-it-was has already gone back into the trunk. We've had a millennium of that — of Celeste flinching from that box full of secrets and me trying (and failing) to help. I've asked her — begged her — to let me inside to help her. But then I realized: Celeste can't see the black trunk inside her mind.

She believes me when I tell her it's there, and she feels its terrors. But just like any human, I suppose, she doesn't know what chases her through the darkness inside."

"She has a repressed memory?" Annabel asked. The thought excited her. Maybe he'd bring her in. Maybe she'd end up with *two* vampire patients, and learn their kind twice as fast.

"*Beyond* repressed," he said. "For vampires, locks form without keys. Mazes self-organize within us, without apparent solutions. I've always believed it's all protective: our minds cordon off parts of themselves simply to protect us from all we accumulate over our rather long lives. The black trunk inside Celeste isn't something she can unlock through hypnosis or anything else a human mentalist might try. It's completely and forever inaccessible — an unflushable irritant like grit in an oyster."

"What does this have to do with Dracula's vial of blood?"

"I turned Celeste so that she wouldn't die," Maurice said, "but I do not know how she came to be so near death. Daisy was nearly killed by Santori's gangsters and Reginald was attacked by my old nemesis Charles's friends. In those cases, I knew what had happened. Through my maker bond with both of them, I was able to understand the visions that put them in trouble, then use my mind as mediator to help them accept it. With Celeste, that wasn't the case. She was already bleeding out, already almost gone. I've seen humans that way before, but something compelled me about her, and I broke my own rule for the first time in a thousand years to save her. But once I'd saved her body, there was nothing I could do for her mind. I didn't know her attackers. I didn't know how it'd happened. Some deep part of Celeste's mind knows: the part that sends her demons in her sleep. The part she's locked away. The part that, if I had context, I might be able to help her open, to get the answers we've always sought. To know who nearly killed her, why, and how."

Annabel waited. "And?"

"There was a vampire who found us five hundred or so years ago. His name was Amadeus Macht. German. He wanted something from us, but he never got to tell us what because someone killed him the day after we met. I never found out who did it. All I know is that shortly before he died, Macht came to us — or to *Celeste*, really, and I just happened to be there at the time. He was a down-on-his luck sort. Reminded me of a hustler on hard times — maybe a guy who'd once lived large, then had a house of cards collapse on his head. He wanted money. A *lot* of money. Whether he planned to extort it out of us or just ask for us to pay, I never found out.

"We met only once, and barely even then. We were traveling and came through a camp. Macht, who happened to be in that camp, must have sensed Celeste's blood. He made himself known that night, acting like just another traveler eager for some company. What I found out later that day, when we went to sleep, was that he'd spiked Celeste's drink with his own blood. Just the tiniest drop — enough to disappear entirely in the mead. Drinking another vampire's blood gives us temporary access to their blood memories, so that night Celeste had visions. I saw her struggling in her sleep and joined her dreams just in time to see the black trunk starting to open. For the first time, someone had slipped her a key."

Annabel sat forward. "Macht was Celeste's maker?"

Maurice shook his head. "I don't know. I helped her navigate the day, dreaming around in circles. I kept that trunk, now ajar, in the corner of my eye, never looking directly at it. I never got more than a feeling from all the dark things her mind had locked inside, so I don't know if Macht was her maker or just someone with knowledge of troubling things from her past. Eventually the trunk closed on its own, because Macht had given her a tiny amount of blood and its intelligence expired as soon as she'd metabolized it.

"We woke that evening to find a note from Macht saying that he knew things we'd spent our lives wondering. He said he had a lot more to offer, and wanted to make a deal. But by the time we found him, he was ash. Someone had ended him — and with him, we'd lost all our answers."

"So the blood that Dracula offered you ..."

"He said it was Macht's," Maurice told her. "How he knew that would mean something to me, I didn't know. How he got it or knew who Macht was — well, *that* I didn't know, either. Remember, I met Dracula in America in 1893, whereas my encounter with Amadeus Macht had been mid-millennium in Europe. Celeste hadn't come with me to America then; she had to hold down the fort back home until I returned. I couldn't talk directly to her to square our stories. I could send letters or telegraphs, but distance strains blood telepathy like a bad phone connection. So I had to decide on Dracula's deal on my own — and I did."

"You took Dracula's deal so you could get your hands on Macht's blood," Annabel said. "Because if you drank it ..."

Maurice nodded. "It was plenty to give me access to everything Macht's memories had to say. I didn't know what those memories were, but I knew from that one tiny sample drop Macht had given Celeste that it was worth seeing. We'd been crushed when we'd found Macht dead. I'd thought for a few shining hours that this was our chance to know the truth and heal Celeste's nightmares, but it'd immediately been taken away. Now, here was that chance again, if I just do as Dracula said."

"So you were willing," Annabel said. "You were willing to snoop around Holmes's castle for Dracula, because if you did, he'd give you the blood."

"And the answers," Maurice said.

SEVEN

TOUR

Tell the truth, I would have done it anyway. Knowing
that Dracula had reached out through other vampires' blood
ties and *made* me curious about Holmes changed nothing.
Even without Dracula's manipulations, I'd grown interested
in him myself. Before I learned it was Dracula's blood
hunch that had dragged me to 63rd and Wallace, I'd had
plenty of time to look around the city, feel its vibe, and get a
baseline sense of its mood. Vampires can't read most
humans' minds, but even without glamouring anyone to
loosen lips, I'd have felt Chicago in its every brick and
window. The city itself breathed a slow sigh of filth and
badness: filth because in those days, there was no concept of
pollution. Badness because its size and growth had spawned
an underbelly — more a simple fact than a tragedy.

So I told Dracula I'd spy on H. H. Holmes for him. I'd
try to learn what I could about the disappearance of
Emeline Cigrande. I told him I'd do it for the vial of blood,
which he'd deliver when I conveyed my findings. But I'd
have still come to the hotel before meeting Dracula, even if

I'd unknowingly felt his influence. The desire was within me. I was simple to move.

Together, with Wyatt occupying Benjamin Pitezel, Dracula and I entreated entry to the castle. I'd already been invited into that human home, and Holmes — always gracious, even with those he'd turned away — re-invited me as well as my new companion. Holmes made no comment about Dracula's absurd outfit, asked no questions about the lateness of our visit or the pointlessness of our inquiry. He did not ask why Dracula, just moments ago, was once again grabbing his head as if he had a headache. Instead Holmes took us back up to that same reception room I'd visited earlier. He offered us brandy and cigars, as if we were honored guests at a supper club rather than unsuitable tenants for his supposedly-booked-solid hotel.

I started the glamour. Holmes smirked: the second part of his broken mind seeing what I was trying and moving to effortlessly deflect it. But then Dracula coaxed out that second half of Holmes's mind and occupied it as well, and for a full hour we worked to influence his mind. It was still a near thing. Holmes's will was strong. His charisma was force enough, almost, to deflect our intention. But then it was over, and Holmes's expression changed, and suddenly he was willing to offer me any room in the building that I wanted. As I'd suspected, there were actually quite a few unoccupied — although if the young gentleman preferred, Holmes told me, he'd be happy to boot any guest from an occupied room as well.

I told him no, no, that wasn't necessary. I'd take a room on the second floor — any that wasn't already in use. Holmes, duly glamoured, was almost pleased. He bade me to stay for as long as I'd like, free of charge. I accepted. I'd planned to stay for up to a year, and how kind it was of the proprietor to make such a long stay easy on my wallet.

When Wyatt was gone and Dracula was gone, I asked Pitezel to take my luggage (a single shoulder bag I'd been lugging) to my room so that Holmes could give me the tour.

The second we were alone, I began to sense a change in Holmes's mood. Outwardly, he was as friendly and charming as ever. Beneath this, though, I could feel an edge. Within an hour of glamouring, Holmes had already stopped being a man filled with genuine pleasure at my company and instead become a man *feigning* pleasure at an unwanted situation. He had the manner of a man bamboozled but unwilling to admit it. He took me around, the glamour barely enough to keep him from throwing me out.

I watched the tailored back of Holmes's jacket as we walked the halls, reminding myself to tread carefully. He was a dichrome, and that meant he almost had two people inside him — a right Jeckyll and Hyde. One half of Holmes kept right on smiling, happy to be my host. But there was another Holmes beneath that I couldn't help thinking saw right through me. *That* Holmes, I suspected, knew everything: that I was a vampire, that I believed the sideshow rumors about this man and this place, that I was not the friend or innocent I pretended to be.

We started on the top floor — the third. There were many guest rooms, but the floorplan was strange. I can't define "strange"; it was a back-of-the-neck, pit-of-the-stomach feeling. Apparently in humans, a vast number of "thinking" neurons live outside of the brain, in the body. In vampires, that's even more true. You learn, after a long enough time undead, that a "gut feeling" isn't a flight of fancy. It's instinct, and it's always worth heeding as much as you'd heed an idea formed consciously.

That's how I felt while walking behind Holmes through those passageways: just ... *wrong*. For one, the hallways kept changing width. The building was a long rectangle — 162 by 50 feet, I later learned — with its short edge facing 63rd. But as you moved away from 63rd, it felt less like traveling the length of Wallace Avenue and more like descending into the bowels of a creature.

Holmes's office was in the northeast corner of the third floor. It was ordinary, but as I made its circuit, I noticed more things amiss. A concealed peephole, for instance, that would have eluded a human but I easily saw with vampire sight. Controls for a gas stove, except that there was no stove in the room. The dimensions were somehow wrong, as if what I saw wasn't the entirety of the room. Curiously, next door to the office was an enormous steel vault — the kind they put in banks, large enough to walk around in. I inquired about it, fascinated by the thing itself, but also by its placement. Why did his hotel contain such a structure at all, yes — but even beyond that, why had he put it on the third floor? This was pre-1900, remember. Getting a giant metal box up that high couldn't have been cheap or easy.

When I asked, fire flashed in Holmes's eyes. I knew not to ask again. I'd told Dracula that Holmes wouldn't simply tell him what he wanted to know about Emeline (that even glamoured, the two halves of a dichrome's mind protect each other), but I now saw that the same applied to my own questions. He wouldn't even have shown me the vault if he'd been in his right mind, and even with my and Dracula's fingers inside his brain, he certainly wouldn't tell me its history.

We moved down to the second floor. Now that I was seeing more than just the reception rooms up front, the oddity of it made my stomach do leaps.

By later count, there were 51 doors on the second floor of Holmes's hotel. However, there were only 35 rooms — and some of those Holmes wouldn't show me like he shouldn't have shown me the vault. Many of the rooms had two or more doors, the second in some leading into opposite hallways and some leading into other rooms. The design was a madman's. Of that floor's nearly three dozen rooms, only a handful were available for rent. And when you rented from Holmes, sometimes you had to go through someone else's room to reach yours.

I'd found the hallways on the third floor unnerving, but the second floor took that feeling to another level. The halls there were often only one person wide. You had to squeeze to pass and the place was full of blind corners. In those tight spaces, Holmes had to stay ahead of me. That was okay. I didn't like the idea of having him behind me.

The corridors twined like a maze. There were go-nowhere passages, doors that opened to blank walls, and seams in the wallpaper where my eye saw gaps and my skin felt drafts. Stairways went nowhere. Hallways changed width, circled back on themselves, and required more than one double-back even from Holmes, who'd built the place. After my questions about the vault, his subconscious was on high alert. He wouldn't open most of the rooms for me other than to show available rentals. When I asked about others, he cited privacy — for the guests, of course, rather than himself.

Despite the hour, we did come across two such guests — one in nightclothes, the other returning from an evening on the town. They were both pretty women under the age of thirty, naive and new to the city. Not that they felt out of place. All the ladies loved Holmes, and he loved them right back. Until they checked out, of course ... or went missing.

One room, I opened without permission. I waited until Holmes was ahead, going on about Chicago and the coming fair. I watched him closely, choosing my moment. When I reached for the knob, my hand shook. It wasn't fear I was feeling. It was unease. It was a sense that everything was wrong, and could quickly become worse.

The room I opened was maybe twelve by eight. It smelled of must and the sour tang of gas. I watched Holmes turn another of those blind corners ahead, then slipped inside. The room was featureless, as if the builder had forgotten to finish it. There were no windows — just an enormous dark closet. No light, either — to search for something here, you'd need a lantern. But the strangest thing was the sense of stillness inside. Even with the door open, I could tell it was mostly or entirely soundproof. Even with air entering from the hall, I could tell there would be no circulation once the door was closed. It was cut off, sealed down. The only feature of interest was a small pipe cut through the wall, almost invisible in a corner. What came out of that pipe? Water?

Holmes was behind me.

"What are you doing?"

"Just exploring."

"How did you enter this room? It was locked."

I looked at the door, suddenly sure he'd slam it and close me inside. The knob was mangled. I'd broken the lock without even realizing it — that's how much my subconscious had wanted to enter.

"Beg pardon, sir," I lied, "but it was not locked when I entered."

Holmes looked at the doorknob, the splintered lock, and then at me. He did not believe me.

"What is this room?" I asked.

"It is a closet."

There was nothing in it. It was in the hotel's middle. I felt claustrophobic just being inside, despite knowing how easy it would be for any vampire to break out.

"Then why is it—?" I began.

But Holmes had his hand on my arm, bringing me out. He closed the door, then continued as if nothing had happened — as if the very air hadn't thickened between us.

"This is my personal room," he said of the chamber next door, sharing the wall through which that strange pipe protruded. "I trust that this one is locked properly." He tried the knob, reminding me that he knew *that* lock wasn't broken.

"How do guests find their way around here?" I asked.

"They follow the hallways, of course."

"But they are so winding."

"They learn," Holmes said, "as they have more mental capacity than goldfish."

"It's so dark. It seems as if you may have brokered more windows?"

"It does seem that way, doesn't it?"

The way Holmes was looking at me, I knew the glamour had already gone gossamer thin. He'd let me stay, because Dracula and I had compelled him. But that was about it.

"The first floor you've already seen," he said, our tour apparently ended.

"But if you wouldn't mind showing me anyway? Your building fascinates me."

Grudgingly, Holmes took me on a tour through the shops. All were closed for the evening. The pharmacy was the largest of them, and for the most part there was nothing unusual. Only one thing caught my attention: At the rear of the tinsmithery was a door with a bench built in front of it. I went to the door, opened it, and peeked behind. There was nothing. Just another door.

"Where does this go?"

"Nowhere. It is an artifact of an error in the design. My fault entirely."

But I wasn't so sure. I'm good at spatial things, and I'd already begun laying out Holmes's building as a 3-D model inside my head. Based on where I'd seen a staircase above, the blocked door had to give stair access. But there was much about the place's space that was wrong, as well. An entire center section of the floorplan was unaccounted for, concealing a small space that ran through all three floors. There was room behind bulkheads that struck me as wide enough for a broom closet, or perhaps a dumbwaiter.

"I see," I said, pretending not to care. "And what is this?"

Moving into the pharmacy, I spied a series of electrical devices. They were bolted into the wall, wires running upward into places unknown.

"Nothing that concerns you."

I took the hint. But there were labels by tiny light bulbs on the equipment, and each seemed to correspond to a section of the hotel. As I watched, a bulb labeled "Second floor rear" lit. At the same time, my vampire ears heard footsteps coming from the same place. They were too quiet for a human to hear, but was that what this device was meant to measure? Had Holmes installed it to tell him when his guests were on the move on the floors above?

I looked around, as someone looking to buy the building might. Holmes watched me, suspicious but pretending to be patient.

"Is there a basement?" I asked.

"Only as much is necessitated by the foundation."

"Still, you must have access to it."

"It's nothing. Merely a crawlspace."

Not true. I'd noticed the give of joists beneath my feet and knew there was a full-sized basement below, not a crawlspace. Unfortunately, my mental 3-D map hadn't shown any place a stairway might be hiding.

"May I see the crawlspace?" I asked.

"There is no reason. It is dangerous. The soil here shifts, making it perilous."

"Just for curiosity, then," I said. "I'm somewhat of a connoisseur of dark spaces." I added a smile to show him that I'd asked the question lighthearted. But Holmes's visage didn't change.

"No guests may enter the basement," Holmes told me.

He tried to smile in turn, but it only touched his mouth and did not rise to his eyes.

"Safety first."

But he'd made a slip, and I planned to investigate it.

He hadn't said "crawlspace" that time — and that time, he'd been telling the truth.

EIGHT
PABST AND SORROW

I slept uneasily.

My sense of disquiet was thick, almost supernatural. Normally, I do not wake from daytime slumber. Even when I do, the sounds that greet me tend to be pedestrian in nature: the light chatter of humans talking, the clack of heels on wood or concrete outside, the passage of horses, carriages, and the occasional automobile.

In Holmes's hotel, I heard something else.

Movement, possibly within the walls. A slow, grinding mumble of gears, chains, or ropes. I did hear voices, but they were anything but pedestrian: whispers that feared being overheard. Distantly, I could hear Holmes, too, as he charmed customers, charmed prospective guests, charmed even creditors who came to collect debts. There was a ghostly stir. Sometimes, a sound like stalking. A sound like *chewing*.

After sunset I made my way to the streets, headed for a planned rendezvous outside the freak show. Despite my general disrespect for Dracula, I was still letting him run things. For now, I had to admit that he knew more than me, and could therefore help me. He knew Chicago; he knew about Holmes enough to have his suspicions; he probably knew more about the disappearances than most. The fact that he was an unmitigated buffoon was something I tried to set aside.

I ran down 63rd Street past the Washington Park Club. At Cottage I went north so I could follow the Midway Plaisance east, then met where the vampire had told me, outside the gate.

He'd told me to join him at 10:08. At 10:08 *precisely*. Ten on the dot was too early; he'd still be performing and didn't like the distraction of knowing others were waiting. 10:15 was too late — we had much to discuss. I considered pitching 10:05 because what the hell was 10:08 to anyone, but Dracula had waved me away.

Eccentric, Dracula called himself. I had another word for it: *douchebag*. I'm not even sure douchebags were invented by then, but that's what he was regardless.

I found the freaks assembled. Every single one of them. Dracula had told me, before he and Wyatt left the hotel last night, that the freaks would be happy to help in any way I could use them. What I hadn't realized was that he'd rallied them like a really weird Justice League. If there was a way to turn these people to good use, I was yet to see it.

In addition to Wyatt, I found Pip and Flip, the Yucatan twins, almost entirely baldheaded save trim little top-knots. They wore house dresses and were very nice to me despite not speaking any language I knew — useful in case our cause needed someone to infiltrate Holmes's barbershop with complaints about haircuts.

There was Unzie the Albino, in case we needed anyone to impersonate Santa Claus.

There was Isaac the Living Skeleton, who I guess was there to remind us to eat more.

The bearded lady was present in case a beard was necessary. Camel Girl, whose knees bent backward, was there for ... well ... I had no idea. Tatiana came with all her tattoos in case we got bored mid-caper and needed something to read. Lastly there was Mike the Headless Chicken. Mike had been living without a head for months, and I think Dracula wanted him around because he was going to die eventually and then we'd have something to eat.

I'd only met a few of the freaks, but as I made the rounds I found them all friendly. They all knew I was a vampire. Dracula had blabbed. It was annoying, because he'd programmed them all to think vampires were all like him.

"Where's your cape?" Tatiana asked me.

"Or your count's medallion?" Unzie said.

Mike the Headless Chicken would have offered something to this exchange, I'm sure, if he'd still had the means to *bawk-bawk*. As it was, he just sort of ran repeatedly into my lower leg.

I looked at a clock. "It's 10:15. He said 10:08."

"Who?" asked Isaac.

"Eugene."

They all looked at each other.

"Dracula," I sighed.

Murmurs of recognition replaced the confusion. Tatiana said, "He's getting his fangs sucked."

"I don't know what that means," I told her.

"Don't you have fangs?"

I didn't want to go further down the rabbit hole. I chose not to respond.

"Well, don't you get them sucked?"

"I don't ... What does that even mean?" I thought it might be a euphemism. Fangs are just teeth. Teeth are enamel. There's no joy in sucking enamel, and I'm not even sure how it'd be done without an extension hose. I assumed he was having something else sucked. But this was Dracula, and he did claim to be a trend-setter.

They were all looking at me. Waiting.

"Well, I guess I'll go back to the hotel?" I sincerely didn't know. But I started to walk, and they all walked with me.

"Just me," I said.

They mumbled. Then Camel Girl said, "What are *we* supposed to do?"

"I don't know. Go home. Stay here."

"There's no show tonight."

"Dracula said he had a show ending at 10pm."

"He calls his sex games 'The Show.'"

I was about to respond to this when either Pip or Flip began pantomiming. Whichever one it was danced a little, then moved around and clapped. I took this to mean that Dracula invited audiences to his shows. Wherein he got his fangs sucked.

I was suddenly struck with the realization that I shouldn't be here. What the hell had I gotten into?

"I'm going to go this way," I said, pointing. We were outside the fence, and everything was still blocked off. People had come early and now just had to wait around. The exposition was highly anticipated, not well planned-for. Without Facebook, people ended up miscommunicating a lot back then.

I walked along the outside of the midway. The freaks came with me.

"Seriously," I said. "I'm going alone."

Isaac cheered this. It's like he didn't understand what I was saying.

I hopped the fence to get away from them. They knew I was a vampire, so I could do it without hesitating. One blink and I was on the other side, free. But they were performers; I'd forgotten that. They simply walked down to the next gate and used their passes to enter.

"You guys don't need to come," I said.

Pip and Flip smiled and nodded.

Now inside the coming fair, we walked down the midway. The Ferris wheel was still in ruins, as if it were in the process of coming down rather than going up. They were still following me. We arrived at a lively gathering where enthusiastic inventors were sharing samples of a new brew called Pabst Blue Ribbon. They must have been sharing generously, too, because those in attendance were *fucked up*.

Someone grabbed my arm. It was a man in a topcoat wearing a bowler hat and a mustache like a walrus's.

"Say boy," he said. "Are you over eighteen? How old are you?"

The yeast on his breath was enough to form colonies. If I were human, I could have gotten drunk off his contact buzz.

"I'm nineteen hundred."

"Nineteen, you say? Funny thing — you don't look a day over seventeen."

"I've avoided work in the coal mines," I explained. This must have been good enough for him because he slapped something in my hand that immediately spilled everywhere. It was beer. Shitty, low-rent, American-brewed beer.

"Down it goes!" my benefactor said to me.

I took a sip. It was like drinking alpaca sweat.

"Delicious, isn't it?"

"Oh hell yeah."

"Have another! They're gratis tonight!"

I wasn't done with my first PBR. Didn't ever need another. "Maybe later," I said.

But he'd already lost interest in me. There was a woman behind him who'd lifted up what looked like five out of seven petticoats, and was threatening to display a tiny flash of ankle. Old-timey boners were everywhere.

The gathering was incredibly drunken. I'd only seen the edge of it, but within a few minutes I and my tail of freaks were in the epicenter. It wasn't just a Pabst give-away; it was actually the inside-the-gate portion of a hullabaloo being run by Buffalo Bill Cody.

Tatiana, the painted lady, came up beside me.

"You seen this before?"

I looked around. Nope, I'd never seen *this* before. *This* — which was overwhelming my disgust circuits more by the second — was exactly what I'd feared when deciding to come to America. Europe was mature; America was barely more than a hundred years old. They were as much wild-lands as civilized, and rumor said that half the nation was still frontier. At the frontier of anything, you got debauchery and lawlessness. You got a few hundred drunk assholes throwing up and fornicating everywhere. Eventually there'd be fights. Not my scene. Not my scene at all.

"Look," Tatiana said.

I followed her finger, seeing an open area just beyond the fence with people riding horses in a circle, choreographing lasso tricks. Indian warriors in full dress were at the edges, one in particular looking ready to scalp the drunk asshole who kept ramming his side.

Then I realized. We weren't just watching a beer give-away and the grope-fest that ensued. We were watching a show — one attended by a very drunken crowd.

"What is it?" I said, inching forward. I had to push through foul-breathed miscreants to see better, owing to my stature. The freaks followed. I could immediately hear the drunks begin to engage them in conversation. Apparently my new friends were a hit on the midway, known for partying as much as for being strange to look at.

The bearded lady, I saw, was knocking back full glasses of beer at a time. Yip and Pip were putting on a dance they'd clearly been asked to perform before. I hadn't noticed Koo Koo the Bird Girl in her duck-shaped shoes and feathered ensemble when we'd left our start point, but there she was now, doing some nineteenth century precursor of breakdancing. As we went, I heard more of the freaks greeted, pulled aside, welcomed like normal people usually only welcome fellow normals.

Twenty feet in and now at the front line of the show, only Tatiana and I remained. I glanced over before taking in the ring. Tatiana would have been plain without all her ink, but with it she was a vision. The normal rules of female modesty either didn't pertain to Tatiana (maybe because ink covered her in the way clothing normally would) or she didn't care. She was in a top low enough to show cleavage, shoulders and arms bare. Her skin, all the way to her shoulder blades, was covered in black and white and fading color.

She answered the question I'd asked earlier.

"It's Buffalo Bill's Wild West Show. Do you know it?"

I shook my head. I didn't want to look away. The spectacle in front of me was uniquely, indelibly American. France had no equivalent. In addition to the horses and Indian warriors, there were men in cowboy hats racing pintos in a circle, swinging loops of rope overhead, making the ropes do tricks. Dust from trampling hooves filled the air. They had only gaslight, but were putting on quite the show anyway.

"And there? See her?"

Tatiana pointed at a woman with long, voluminous brown hair.

"Annie Oakley. You want to steal a lady's purse? Don't steal hers. She'll perforate you from five blocks away."

I watched for a while, fascinated. I hadn't scoped the main body of the fair yet, mostly because the gates would remain closed until May 1. Still, I'd seen the so-called "White City" from a distance, and had tried not to be impressed. I'd managed, with effort. But this little ring of horses and humans — just outside the gate as if tossed together — entranced me far more.

"They were denied," Tatiana told me.

I turned to look at her.

"Buffalo Bill," she explained. "Can you believe that? Just about the most popular live show around, and the organizers told Bill Cody he couldn't add his show to the spectacle inside. They said it was too low-brow. The fair is supposed to be *high* brow." She laughed. "We snatched a copy of a site plan. Remind me to show it to you sometime. The shop order goes bar, dance hall, bordello, bar, bordello. It's all whores and drinking; don't let the ladies' do-gooder committee fool you. They've been fighting just about every sideline exhibit at the exposition and winning none of it. This is where some fool got to make their stand: Keeping Buffalo Bill and all the money he could bring *out* of the Columbian Exposition. So do you know what he's going to do instead?" She pointed at the ground, then stomped once for emphasis. "He's going to set up right here. Just outside the gate. See those tents? That's all they need. This way, he gets all the attention the fair offers but doesn't have to cut them in on the profits. Smart, right?"

I nodded. But I wasn't here for Buffalo Bill. Wasn't here for any of this.

I moved on, extracting myself from the crowd. Tatiana followed. When we were clear of the PBR crew and into a bit of quiet, I looked back and realized we'd lost the rest of the freaks seemingly for good. Tatiana was still there, walking beside me with all the normality she might have had if she didn't look like a walking newspaper.

She said, "Eugene says you're here for Holmes."

I looked over. I smiled. Couldn't help it. She'd called him Eugene.

"I'm here for myself."

"But you're staying at the castle."

"For my own reasons."

"He told us you were on the trail of Emeline."

Asshole. I corrected her: "I am here for the expo. He and I made a deal, but only because it suited me. I'd already focused in on your man Holmes. He leaves a psychic stink, is all I can say to describe it. That stink drew me to his building before I met that idiot in a cape. I will see what I can find out about this Emeline, but she's not the reason I'm here."

"He likes me, you know."

"Who?"

"Holmes. I know that Dracula ... *Eugene* ... told you Holmes keeps coming by the midway. To the freak show in particular. But the fair's not even open. Who comes to a freak show when there's barely a show? But he doesn't just watch our little song and dance. He watches it *over and over and over*. Everyone says it's because he's sweet on me."

"Not sure that's something I'd be as proud of as you seem to be."

"Hey, flattery is flattery, even if it is from a weirdo. I mean, look at me. Tell me I'm *not* seeking attention."

I looked. I thought that was a remarkably self-aware thing to say, and not anything I'd have expected her to realize. Tattoos in the 1890s were for sailors and tribesmen. Normal men didn't get them and women *definitely* didn't — at least not in the quantities Tatiana had. Of course some part of her craved attention. She just wasn't supposed to see it so plainly.

We walked on.

"Where are you going, anyway?" Tatiana asked.

"Nowhere. I'm only walking."

"Not toward the midway. Not toward the heart of the expo."

"No point. The expo isn't open yet."

"Not back to your lodging, either," she went on. "Are we leaving? If we're going far from the grounds, I may want to run back for a coat."

I looked at her. She wasn't cold. She was thinking of modesty. On the midway, the freaks were celebrated. Away from it, Tatiana looked different enough to be frightening.

"*We* aren't going anywhere," I said. "*I* am going wherever my feet take me."

"But what about Dracula?"

"What about him? I only came tonight because he promised information. He's not here, so no information. It doesn't matter. I'm in the castle already. I can do this on my own."

A voice inside me said, *What do you mean by "this"?* I wasn't sure. I hoped she'd miss it, and she did.

But she wasn't wrong about my direction. I really *was*

headed somewhere specific, and I didn't know where that specific place was. It felt like meandering without purpose, except for one tiny difference: Every once in a while, I'd take a random turn and think, *Nope, wrong way.* Which shouldn't have been possible if I was truly wandering without reason.

So I tuned in to the feeling, ignoring Tatiana as she stayed close, not breaking off, not going back for that jacket. I focused on the strange force compelling me, putting one foot in front of the other.

Right. Left. Straight ahead. I found myself looping back toward the main body of the fairgrounds: the Idaho-shaped property along Lake Michigan that connected to the midway like a single arm. We'd circled around an obstruction on autopilot, now very near the fences. And that's when I heard someone crying, and spied the old woman.

Tatiana looked from her to me and said, "You feel something from her, don't you?"

I did. It took me a few calibration minutes to understand, but I definitely did. Vampire sensation is a curious thing. Although we can't read human minds, we *can* feel their energies — especially if they're strong enough. Although we aren't psychic in the usual sense, most of us are excellent at pattern recognition. I suppose I'd been feeling this woman's grief for days, along with the other emotions inside this filthy, crime-ridden city. I just hadn't recognized it until it'd harmonized with Dracula's blood hunches and blood obsession for Emeline, plus the now-familiar sense of Holmes's "psychic stink."

I stepped closer. Whatever had happened — whoever this woman was — she had something to do with what I was after. Something to do with why I was here. Something, I knew, having to do with Holmes.

I squatted in front of her. Tatiana remained standing. When the woman looked up, she did not show surprise. I felt plenty of surprise, pushing it down. In truth, she was not old. It was only sadness that had made her seem that way.

"Who are you?" she asked.

Strange question, for a man who's done nothing more than show up in front of you.

"My name is Maurice. What's your name?"

"Mamie Conner."

I stood, listening to the wind, mulling the name like I might sample a wine. It struck me as familiar — or near to familiar? But no; I realized it wasn't Mamie's name I knew so much as the *feeling* of her — or the feeling she'd spent some time chasing on her own. Whatever my sense was, I'd swear it was on the air itself. Something from that miasma of blood intuition in the air — from Dracula's mind, perhaps, but more likely the voice of the vampire underground itself. My people hear things. We *always* hear things. We seldom interfere in human lives unless it is to feed. But that sense ... what was behind it?

"What's wrong?" I asked, coming up empty.

"My friend, Julia. I cannot find her."

I thought: *Julia.* I knew that name, too.

I stood, looking around. The woman was young; her friend may have been younger still. She was fretting like a woman who'd misplaced a child — but only after searching for so long that giving up was literally the only option. But I saw nothing.

"You will not find her that way," she said, still sitting on the curb.

"Why?"

"Because she went missing over a year ago."

Tatiana squatted now, taking her hand. To the woman's credit, she didn't flinch from the freak's grip. Instead, she took it warmly. Any port in a storm of sorrow, it seemed.

"What made you come looking now, if it happened so long ago?" I asked.

"I thought she might merely be unwell. That her letters may have gone wayward, or she might have found herself short on time to write them. She had a crisis, see, and ..."

I sensed reticence in the woman — something she was holding back out of modesty. I looked into her eyes with light glamour and said, "It's okay. You can tell me."

She softened as if plied by drink. Then she said, "I had a letter from Julia before the new year. Before the *last* new year, in December of '91. She'd been staying in Chicago with her husband and daughter, but in one of her last letters she told me she'd left Ned. She said she and Pearl were happy in their many rooms."

"But?"

"But Julia had one trouble: the abortion."

I looked at Tatiana. Tatiana looked at me. In an age when people didn't speak of divorce above a whisper, the idea of an abortion was a million times more scandalous. It wasn't just the act; it was all that surrounded it. From context I knew that Julia was married to a man, Ned, and that she'd shacked up with another man instead. What Mamie had just said broached the topics of sex, infidelity, and the general notion of female genitals even before abortion entered the picture. She'd never have said such a thing — let alone to a stranger — without my fingers inside her mind.

Mamie went on, sensing none of our discomfort.

"She was always a faithful correspondent. It's not like Julia to fail to reply to letters, or to fail to proactively write them to friends and family. I have not relocated. She knows how to reach me. I believed I knew how to reach her as well, though possibly she relocated and I'm mistaken. Or so it seems. I have already visited the rooms she was staying at, and according to the proprietor, Julia checked out and fully paid just before the time she ceased corresponding with me." She looked up, and we could both see the tears welling her eyes. "Something's happened to her. I just *know* it!"

"Where was she staying?" Tatiana asked. "The address you had — the place you visited to speak to the proprietor. Where was it?"

But we already knew, didn't we?

"63rd and Wallace," she said. "The hotel they call the castle."

NINE

CORRIDORS

THERE WAS a knock on my chamber window. I looked out to see Dracula clinging to a metal conduit bolted to the outside of the building.

I opened it. "What."

"I can't get in."

"How tragic."

"I tried to meet you at the gate like we said. With the other freaks."

I wasn't sure I liked his use of "other." I wasn't a freak. Not his kind, anyway. "We were all there at 10:08. Did you actually think you'd be there at that exact time, or were you just being a dick?"

"I'm sorry. I got held up. I was getting my fangs sucked."

"What does that mean?"

"You've never had your fangs sucked?" he asked.

"No. I don't even understand how that would work."

"Well, what you do is—"

I held up a hand. "And I'm not asking."

I hadn't looked up. I was at the room's writing desk, thinking how much the ink in the inkwell looked like blood in the dim, midnight light. I hadn't eaten enough. I'd meant to; that's probably half of where my feet had been taking me. But after meeting Mamie, I'd been driven in new ways and had only snacked as an afterthought. One quick wino, devoured like a modern protein bar. I barely had time to enjoy it.

"She was really hot," said Dracula.

"Who was?"

"The girl sucking my fangs. So you understand. It's not like I could just leave early because I had a commitment. It's not like I'd committed anything to anyone."

I ignored him.

"Did I mention my fang-sucker brought a friend? Because she did. There were two of them. And don't even ask about the waffle."

"Jesus. Okay, I definitely won't."

Dracula rattled the windowsill. "Let me in."

"Okay. Fine. Come on in."

He pushed at the open space. There wasn't a screen, but he made no more progress than he would have against glass.

"I can't. Holmes must have revoked his invitation."

I wondered how that had happened? Maybe I'd found Holmes when I'd gotten back, managed a tiny glamour on my own, and suggested he tell the air he was revoking access permission for all vampires except for me.

"Go get him, Maurice."

"Nah."

"You're angry," Dracula said.

"Maybe eventually. Right now I'm just annoyed. Turns out there's a problem with my room. This one's got an asswipe at the window."

"You should just tell him to re-invite me and get it over with," Dracula said. "I can stay here all night."

I reached through the open window, put my palm against his face, and pushed hard enough that the pole he was clinging to ripped from the building. He shot toward the street on the top of the severed conduit like a pole vaulter coming up short. The impact was enough to create a Dracula-shaped indentation in the brick. He lost his grip and the pipe rebounded most of the way.

He climbed again, far unsteadier this time.

"You need my help, Maurice."

"For what?"

"Tatiana told me you have new information on Holmes. Another woman he may have captured or killed. If you want background, I'm the only one who has it. I've made a study."

"Yet you've never investigated on your own."

"I told you. I *can't* do it on my own. *I'm a celebrity.* Everyone would be watching everything I did."

He was rubbing his head again. Vampires weren't supposed to get headaches.

Not that I cared. I said, "Uh-huh."

"'*Julia Smythe,*'" Dracula recited, apparently told by Tatiana." Do you even know who she is?"

That irked me. I'd come here with just "Julia," then snooped in Holmes's files until I'd found mention of a Smythe. Dracula hadn't even needed to snoop. He'd come here knowing what I'd discovered.

"Julia was another of his paramours," Dracula told me, moving to climbing the building's brick ledge. "Maybe his first in the city. Smythe came here with her husband and daughter, Ned and Pearl. Holmes wooed her. Ned left with his dick between his legs like a little cuckholded bitch."

"A lot of sympathy for Ned, I see," I said.

"Hey. Julia was out of his league. I've seen pictures."

"So you didn't know her."

"No I didn't *know* her. Why would I *know* her?" Dracula acted like I, not he, was the annoying one. "I know because I asked around. I did some glamouring. People say Holmes knocked her up, talked her into an abortion, and after that she wasn't seen again. He was going to perform the procedure himself. I'm guessing the needle slipped. Is that how they do it? I've always imagined a needle."

I didn't want to hear it. As much gore as I've handled in my long life, I've never been comfortable with human medicine. If a human is eviscerated for a kill, I can at least understand it: When your chest cavity is violently opened, you die. But medicine? Medicine opens people up *while they're still alive*. It's creepy. Especially that footage you sometimes see of a person having brain surgery while conscious. *Yeah, I'm having this conversation with my brain out. What of it?* Chills.

"You need me, Maurice," Dracula said.

I closed the window.

"Maurice?" Muffled now.

"Maurice isn't here."

"Maurice!"

I drew the blinds, too. Then I stood up and left the room, deciding now would be a good time to use the restroom. There were no lights; either Holmes left them dark after a certain time or he'd failed to turn on the gas. No matter. I can see just fine if there's any light at all, even if it's just the glow of a firefly.

I walked the hall's length, then turned where I thought the washroom was. I was wrong, though, so I walked another length. At the end of this final hall was a dead end. The hallway just stopped, no doors close.

Weird.

I turned back. I saw an oil lantern coming, but not before it was right on me. The hallway's convolutions trapped light like the exit of a darkroom. The walls were papered, but the finish was matte and the colors were dark.

I turned right into someone else. She jumped and almost dropped the lantern. We'd run nearly smack into one another, and one of us would need to back up (or enter a room) to let the other pass. That's how narrow the hallways were.

"Oh! Beg pardon," the woman said. She put a hand to her bosom. "I must have given you a fright."

Clearly, she was the frightened one. Anyone would be, up here in the dark. I wanted to ask her why she was up so late, but it seemed imprudent. She had an inch of independence to her, but it was clearly a new thing. She struck me as a sweet, smooth-skinned country girl who'd come to the city and begun to learn its ways ... but who hadn't yet appreciated those ways enough to be tough, to be safe.

"It's no problem."

She looked over her shoulder. "I know this is silly, but I seem to have misplaced my room."

I smiled. I picked it up, pitching my voice into soothing, near-glamour tones.

"I'm sure it's right where you left it," I said. "What's the number?" But that was absurd. The rooms weren't numbered. That would be too logical. So before she could try to answer, I added, "I mean, do you remember what it was near?"

"There was a vent in one of the walls. I could hear air circulating. And it was somewhere near the laundry chute."

"Laundry chute? I haven't seen one."

"Oh, yes. I sometimes hear Henry dropping laundry down it at night."

Curious. *Laundry chute? At night?* What's more, she wouldn't call Holmes by his first name unless they were good friends or intimate — not simply innkeeper and guest. My bet, given Holmes's magnetic manner and the tales I'd heard, was on the latter.

"I'm Maurice Toussant," I told her. "I'm staying just down the hall. Maybe I can help you find your chambers."

She smiled, gaze downcast, almost blushing. *Silly*, her eyes seemed to say. She took the hand I'd offered. Hers was small and cold. "Edna Van Tassel."

I led her to her room, which she found easily once oriented.

She smiled, thanked me, and we parted.

It was good, my first meeting of Edna Van Tassel.

But as things turned out, that first meeting was also our last.

TEN

LAUNDRY

THE NEXT EVENING, just after dusk, I went to check on
Edna. I found her door open, her bed stripped. Ben Pitezel
was carrying a load of sheets, dropping them into a rolling
hamper.

"Maid duty?" I asked.

"We're a small operation," he told me. "I wear many
hats."

"Just never indoors," I said.

He looked at me.

"It was a joke. About a man wearing his hat indoors?"

"Oh, yes. Quite."

I saw that he was jittery. Nervous. I'm not good at being
cordial, but I thought my mild joke had been on-point. He
was acting like he hadn't really heard it, that he'd taken it for
serious. I'd glamoured Pitezel same as I'd glamoured
Holmes, albeit with much less effort. Still, despite the ease
with which I found myself able to influence the man, my
questions found him empty. He was hiding something ...
desperately. Humans can overcome a vampire's will if their
defenses are strong enough — and on the topic of Holmes

and the hotel, the otherwise soft-headed Benjamin Pitezel was an iron box.

"Is everything okay, Mr. Pitezel?"

"Everything is fine."

"Have you spoken with Ms. Van Tassel this morning?"

"Who?"

"Edna Van Tassel. It's her room you're cleaning."

"Oh. Yes. Well, she checked out this morning."

"She's gone?"

"Yes. Back to Iowa."

"Just like that?"

"Why not? This is Chicago. The curious come and go."

"But ..." I couldn't articulate why that didn't make sense to me. After plumbing what felt like a million human minds, I've gotten pretty good at reading intention. There was no reason for Edna to have told me her plans last night, nor for me to have inquired. Still, who came to Chicago on the eve of a legendary exposition and left before it began? I'd seen her to her door, and peeking past her I hadn't seen suitcases open or other signs of tidying up and shutting down. Of course, there was every reason in the world for her to have been planning her exit and for me not to have known it, but it didn't feel right. It felt outright wrong.

"Good day to you," Pitezel said as he wheeled the basket of linens past, headed for the staircase.

"Taking that dolly down the stairs?" I called.

"There's no other way. I'll manage."

"What about the laundry chute?"

"The what?"

"The laundry chute, sir. You could simply drop the linens into the basement."

He looked puzzled. "There's no laundry chute in the hotel, sir. We do not even have a wash basin or a mangle.

Dr. Holmes sends it out." I noticed he didn't say, *And we don't have a basement, either.*

"Has he always sent the linens out for washing?"

Pitezel shrugged, less to suggest ignorance than to wonder why I was still asking questions.

"Yes, sir. Why?"

I shook my head. "No reason." Pitezel eyed me. I turned and went back to my room.

Then I buttonhooked, took a wrong path, and ended at a door that opened to a blank wall. It took me a few turns to find my way in the maze again. The loss of direction unnerved me. I'm not normally claustrophobic, but I felt it then. If I were human, just being in those strange hallways would have given me the creeps.

When I found Edna's room again, Pitezel was nowhere to be seen.

I entered, listening and looking to make sure the coast was clear. I could hear minute stirrings from the other rooms, but I could tell the noises were being made by guests.

I looked around, getting the lay.

The room was small but homey. The bed wasn't yet re-made, but the rest of the room was tidily in place. It struck me not just as organized, but also dusted. Every surface had been wiped clean, the scent that of an astringent cleanser. There was a wooden desk as in my room, but the entire inkwell had been replaced, a few pages of creamy paper inside, edges straight and brand new. I put my hand on the chair as if I might feel body heat (Ms. Van Tassel, sitting down to pen a letter announcing her departure) but of course I felt nothing but cool wood. I put a hand to the bed, naturally feeling nothing there, either.

I made a slow circuit, noting that her room was in the building's center and had no window. Beneath the bed I found a single woman's shoe. Just one. Had she left wearing only one shoe? I supposed it was possible the singleton was from another pair or left by the last guest, but modest women of the time seldom had more than one pair. Given the attention paid to cleaning the room elsewhere, it seemed strange that Pitezel and crew would have missed a shoe from two guests ago.

I picked it up, set it down. Then I went to the walls.

I put my ear to one and listened.

Through it, I heard the small ticking noises any building makes in wind or when temperature changes, nothing more. After a few seconds I moved to the rear wall, heard the sigh of moving air, and took it to be the vent she'd mentioned. I was just about to put my ear to the third wall when a tall figure in a five-button traveling coat appeared at the door.

"Oh. Mr. Holmes," I said, seeing him. "I was merely looking for Ms. Van Tassel."

"It's actually *Doctor* Holmes," he said.

He entered. Touched the chair I'd felt earlier, high up, on the back. With a small motion of his hand, he turned it a little. The chair squeaked.

"You knew Ms. Van Tassel?" Holmes asked me.

"We met last night."

"Well. Rest assured, you will not find her inside that wall."

I pulled my ear from the wallpaper, feeling ridiculous.

"You are a curious man, Mr. Toussant," he said.

"How so?"

"Setting aside your predilection for listening to plaster, you seem only to move about at night. I wanted to invite you to lunch, then to coffee. Both times I knocked, you did not answer."

"I was out."

Holmes smiled patronizingly. Somehow, he knew I hadn't left.

"Then we must lunch tomorrow. I know a fine spot in the park."

"I'm afraid I'm otherwise engaged tomorrow," I told him.

"The next day, then."

"Also engaged."

"At any point, perhaps. You may name the day, so long as the sun is shining. The park is so lovely during the daytime, whereas it's my opinion that the ugliness of Chicago comes out at night. There are those who walk the streets at all hours, of course, but you never know who might be out in the darkness. You never know what fate might befall you."

"Curious," I said. "I ran into a woman just yesterday whose friend went missing."

"That *is* curious."

"Not far from here," I added. "The missing friend's name was Julia."

Holmes's face gave no sign. I wished I could glamour him to do more than grudgingly allow my presence. His mind was too strong — too broken — to allow his expression to give him away.

"Well now. That is a pity. But those who come and go in this growing city do tend to be bold by nature. Rulebreakers. Defiers of convention. It does not surprise me anymore when they flit off on a whim, or when they fail to inform others of their movements."

"Is that what happened with Ms. Van Tassel?"

He shrugged. "She paid her rents. She kept her rooms clean. It is not my business to where she goes next." He shifted. "You have not answered my invitation."

"To lunch?"

"To lunch in the sun," he clarified.

We stared at each other.

"Well then," he said, breaking the stalemate. "Perhaps when you are ready, you will let me know."

"Perhaps."

I moved to go.

"Mr. Holmes?"

"*Doctor* Holmes."

"What is beyond this wall?" I pointed where I'd been listening.

"Nothing."

"How can there be nothing? Everything is something. Everywhere is somewhere."

He gave another of those patronizing smiles. "Yes, of course. What I meant is that there's nothing that would interest you. There are utilities beyond that wall. Pipes for plumbing. Lines for the gas lights. A vent, for septic gasses."

That's not all I'd heard, I'd swear it. To my ears, it had the echo of a larger space — empty, not stuffed with tubes.

"Will that be all, Mr. Toussant?" he asked.

I thought for a minute about my options. Then I nodded, and turned one more time to go.

"But Mr. Toussant?"

I stopped.

"I'd like to set your mind at ease. You seem concerned about Ms. Van Tassel. I can assure you, with my very breath, that she was well and in good spirits when she left us this morning. She was merely looking for the next adventure, as so many young people are these days."

Young people. I considered the doctor. He was no more than thirty himself, at the very most.

"I'm sure," I said, not sure at all.

"Perhaps you frightened her off. Perhaps if you hadn't engaged her in the middle of the night, she'd still be here with us."

That stopped me cold. I looked in the doctor's soothing blue eyes. I'd heard a taunt, but his eyes betrayed nothing but compassion, the very absence of guile.

"Hopefully it won't need to happen again," Holmes said.

He walked past me, patting me twice on the shoulder as he went, and was gone.

ELEVEN
DEADLOCKED

Annabel raised her head to find Maurice looking at her. She didn't think he'd spoken, but right now he seemed like a man waiting for an answer.

She looked down, as if the answer might be there. She saw that her notepad was covered with doodles that had nothing whatsoever to do with Maurice or his story — doodles, disturbingly, that she had no memory of drawing. Considering the depth and quality, however, it seemed impossible that she could have drawn them while also paying attention.

Sketches of tall men in suits holding tommy guns. Of barrels leaking viscous fluid she knew was blood. Sketches, frankly, that Annabel wasn't artistic enough to draw under ordinary circumstances.

"I'm sorry," she said. "What?"

"Are you paying attention?"

"Yes. Of course." But she was equal parts flustered and confused. Seeing those drawings that looked like the work of someone else unnerved her, so she ripped the offending pages from her book and crumpled them in one hand. His tone bothered her, so she looked up and smiled. This was a mistake. She felt as if he could see right through her.

"What did you just rip out of that book?"

"Nothing."

"Can I see?"

"It's personal." Blushing now. Annabel could feel the heat in her cheeks.

"But this is my session," Maurice countered. "Personal *about me.*"

The second voice in Annabel's head seemed to feel partially (perhaps entirely) responsible, so it rushed to her aid. It whispered: *Go on the offense.*

Out loud, Annabel said, "I have my own methods of treating patients, but that is my business and my business alone. I would not presume to tell you whether or not to go to Chicago in the 19th century, so please don't presume to tell me how to do my job."

Maurice leaned back with his hands up, surrendering. "Sure. Of course. I'm sorry."

She'd better follow that up with something good. Fortunately, despite the doodles, she was quite sure her mind hadn't gone wandering. She remembered every nuance of everything Maurice had said — more detail, in fact, than she normally recalled. It was as if she'd slipped into photographic memory, but the memory in question had been Maurice's instead of her own. She felt like she'd been there in those cramped, dark hallways — perfect places for a stalker to surprise his prey in the dead of night. She could practically imagine Edna's clothing and face. Then, when Maurice and Holmes had had their standoff in Edna's empty room the next evening, Annabel thought she could hear and see every nuance of that as well.

"You were telling me about talking to Holmes," she said.

"That's right."

"And it almost sounded like he knew you were a vampire."

Maurice thought, then laid back. He sighed. "I don't know if he did. That's certainly the way he acted, but we never really got to the part where he could press the point, before he'd have known otherwise. The things he said ..." Another sigh. "Well, who invites someone to lunch, specifically in the daytime sun? It felt like a threat, but the irony is that he was the one who should have had everything to fear."

"But he didn't."

Maurice considered again. The answer, when he gave it, seemed to surprise him. "Actually, come to think of it, no. I don't think Holmes was ever afraid of me. Some part of his mind knew what I was, but whether that part had informed his conscious mind, I didn't know. He must have sensed power in me, because I made no effort to hide it. But no. He was never afraid."

"Should he have been?"

"What do you mean?"

"You're a vampire, now with what sounds like a third woman missing. You have a soft spot for the fairer sex, Maurice. Every story you've told me, except for Reginald's, involves strong women. Sometimes they started out strong and sometimes vampirism *made* them strong. Jess, in your story from last visit ..."

"I know. She didn't want my help. Or need it."

"But still you tried. Maybe it's sexist or maybe it's chivalrous. Given your history, I'll assume your intentions are the latter. I have no reason to believe that in 1893, in an age of chivalry, you would not have felt the same." Annabel tapped her pad, upon which she'd told herself she'd make only notes, no drawings. It was fresh and unmarked. "Did you ever find Edna Van Tassel?"

He didn't answer. That part of the story was still coming.

"There's something I don't understand, Maurice," Annabel said.

"What?"

"Why didn't you kill him, then and there?"

Maurice turned toward her. "What do you mean by that?"

"Exactly what I said. Dr. H. H. Holmes was a serial killer. I looked him up after you mentioned the fair and a man named Holmes last week." Or had she? She remembered getting all that information about Holmes, but not deciding to go after it. In her memory it was almost as if she'd been forced to look up what she had rather than choosing to do so, *Clockwork Orange* style. "He killed at least nine people. Maybe a good deal more. It's possible that you were the first person who encountered Holmes and knew him for what he was, plus had the power and autonomy to stop him. So why didn't you?"

"I ... I wasn't sure. Evidence of his crimes wasn't uncovered until—"

"Oh, come on," Annabel interrupted. *"You knew.* You knew because the freaks told you and because you'd run across three women who went missing after staying in his hotel. But most of all, you knew because you could *feel* it. You've already called him 'evil.' You've said more than once that he drew you from all the way across Chicago with his 'psychic stink.' You knew what he was. Not by a court's standards, maybe, but plenty by your own. So why did you keep playing games with him? Why didn't you force the issue? *Why didn't you kill him,* Maurice?"

"Are you, Doctor, suggesting your patient should have chosen murder?"

"Please," Annabel said. "The first time you were here, you told me you slaughtered the entire vampire Mafia."

"That was in the '20s. This was almost forty years earlier."

"And you'd never, before then, embraced vigilante justice?"

The room sat in silence. Finally Maurice said, "What you're suggesting — that I may have dealt poorly with Holmes — has plagued me for over a century. You searched for Holmes online? God knows I've done it often enough. When I met him, his crimes were just beginning. The worst came later. If I'd have done what I knew I should have, as you said, those horrors never would have happened. But it wasn't that simple at the time. I swear to you it wasn't. History is never clear in the moment. Believe me — I wish I'd had foresight enough to kill Hitler, too. I definitely had the means."

"So you just ... *investigated,*" Annabel said.

"What else could I do? I felt that something was wrong with Holmes, but wasn't sure. That's another thing you start to realize when you visit as many glamours and blood memories as I have: Almost everyone has a dark side, but only some people act on it. Holmes was creepy and a womanizer, but beyond that I couldn't know the rest. That's why I was poking around: to find out for sure. It's the real reason I stuck with Dracula's mission. The vial of blood answers eventually just became a bonus. I needed to know beyond a reasonable doubt. But there was also another reason I didn't kill him, too."

"And what reason was that?"

"I didn't know which victims he might have been holding and where he might have been keeping them. The building struck me as full of secret hiding places, but Holmes also took long trips out of the city, and rumor was that disappearances surrounded him there, too. You've seen *Silence of the Lambs?* Or *Dirty Harry?* Or even *The Cell?* It was like that. When the killer is the only person who knows how to find the missing, you have to think twice before cutting them out of the picture."

Annabel sat back, recrossing her legs. "But Holmes maybe knew about you. Knew the sun was bad for you, and based on what you've said he must have had some clue you were onto him. You were staying at his hotel, as much at his mercy as those young women. You even said your room had a window."

He sat up, shaking his head to explain. "Only because the alternative was a room with a peep hole. Guests never noticed them, but my eyes could pick up the glint. Holmes had peep holes all over the hotel, mostly in the interior rooms because that was where he could trap his victims where they wouldn't be able to escape. On our little tour, I realized I'd have to choose between a window and surveillance by my host. I chose the former, and simply draped it with all the blankets I had."

"But he might have come in during the day," Annabel said. "All he'd have needed to do was to walk in and rip the blankets from the window. From what I read on Wikipedia, I don't even think he'd flinch from using a stake."

"He was glamoured. Imperfectly, but glamoured nonetheless. Pitezel was easy; he'd do what I told him. Holmes's glamour was more like pouring water into a colander. Dracula's and my influence (it always took both of us) trickled out of him from the moment we refreshed our glamour. But as long as we kept getting to him, he couldn't hurt me — including hiring *other* people to hurt me. Until then, it was more like a standoff than control. I'm convinced Holmes knew exactly what we were doing to him, but was powerless to stop it. So we glamoured and he fought it and we glamoured him again. We were like a pair of adversaries pointing guns, neither quite able to pull the trigger. I knew Holmes was a killer and Holmes knew I was ... well, he knew I was *something*. My darkness didn't bother or frighten him at all. Looking back, he may even have admired me. We were foes, but he may have felt I was an ally. I was made of darkness. And so was he."

Annabel took notes, pleased to see that none of those subconscious doodles had returned. "So you knew he was a murderer but couldn't kill him. He knew you were a vampire or something like one, but he couldn't kill you, either."

Maurice nodded. That didn't feel like enough to Annabel, but it wouldn't be the first time Maurice had withheld something from her. She felt sure there had to be another reason Maurice had kept his hands off Holmes, but she could wait for that piece of the puzzle to unfold. If past experience was any guide, Maurice would tell her later in the story ... or she'd find a way to dig it out of him.

"So what happened next?" she asked.

"*Life,*" Maurice answered. "Holmes stayed obnoxiously close to me after that day in Edna's room. I could nose around, but never more than that. It was the most delicate game of cat and mouse, but I couldn't shake the feeling that he had a dozen hostages squirreled away and starving somewhere. The minute I broke down a door, we'd have to clear the decks between us. If that happened, he'd skip town while I was sleeping in my room, perhaps just until the glamour wore off and he could come back to try and kill me. Perhaps he'd never return, glamour or no glamour. Or I'd kill him. Either way, I wouldn't get what I wanted — which in this case, was information about anyone still in danger, unable to save themselves. I couldn't make him talk, and thanks to his monumental repression, I couldn't make Pitezel talk, either. We were stuck."

"What about Dracula?"

"He was as stuck as I was. We tried to learn more, but Holmes always outfoxed us. I can move like a whisper, but somehow Holmes always knew when I was watching."

Annabel thought, wondering where to go next. She already knew, thanks to the internet, that Holmes had survived until 1896, at which point he'd been hanged by the state. The story ended how it ended, and dwelling on ways Maurice had failed to prevent the inevitable would help nobody. Therapy with Maurice wasn't time travel. All she was hearing was a twist on history. All she'd do, if she kept harping on maybes and should-haves, would be to deepen her patient's guilt.

"So you just stayed at the hotel?" she asked.

"Stayed. Observed. Talked a few sweet young ladies *out* of staying. All I could really do was to glamour people nearby for clues and wait, deterring whoever I could. Plus, there was Dracula's mystery to attend to. I needed to find out what happened to Emeline Cigrande if I wanted that vial of blood he'd teased me with, and for that I needed Holmes alive."

Annabel didn't make a note, even though she wanted to. Her note would have come off as cynical and the thought was something she didn't want to commit to paper. It was this: *Had Maurice kept Holmes alive so he could fulfill*

Dracula's bargain and get the blood? Was that his motive more than human safety? Maurice wasn't cruel, but he was more or less immortal. It wasn't possible for immortals to fully empathize with the loss of mortal life. They could try, but they'd never feel it as much as a mortal would. Just not part of their experience.

"I'm sorry," Maurice said. "What was that?"

"I didn't say anything."

"I thought you just ..." He turned, looking around the room as if for an unseen speaker. "Never mind."

This time, Annabel didn't think anything. He couldn't hear her thoughts, could he?

"So you waited," she said. "You bided your time."

"Yes. I visited with the freak show. I kept Dracula in the loop, partially because I wanted to make sure he didn't welch on our deal and partly because I needed his help to keep glamouring Holmes. I thought Dracula was an idiot, but we had the same mission. He wanted me to find information on Emeline. After talking a few more times to Mamie Conner, I became obsessed with finding info on Julia Smythe — plus, now, Edna Van Tassel. We just wanted to know, and to stop whatever might be happening from happening again."

Maurice sighed, maybe with regret, and went on. "Holmes was smart. Brilliant, really. He was a closed box and he'd turned Pitezel into one. He collected no trophies from his victims — and, for the forensics of the time, left no trace. It's as if he saw me coming and built safeguards against me. That meant that if there was evidence to be had, it was in the building itself. But until I found a way to pry without leaving traces of my own, we had a standoff. My glamour could only keep him from moving against me, nothing more. Looking back, the time I spent seems foolish. But at the time ... well ... I did the best I could."

"Everyone does the best they can," Annabel told him. "I know your intentions were good."

Maurice sat back.

"So what came next?" Annabel asked.

And Maurice said, "The fair."

TWELVE
MEASUREMENTS

Not long after our little standoff in Edna's room, the hotel got a new reception girl. Officially, she was Holmes's personal stenographer. Everyone (which by then meant me and the freaks, who followed the castle's goings-on like a Dickens serial) was sure she was closer to a plaything. Minnie Williams was bright-eyed and warm, far too nice to be around Holmes as he actually was, versus how he appeared to the world. She'd been an actress, come to Chicago for the fair, and bunked with Holmes as he schemed to get his hands on her money.

"Tell her to run," said Tatiana, the painted lady.

"Warn her away," agreed Isaac, the Human Skeleton.

The creepy twins nodded. Seeing as they didn't know English, I wondered what they were nodding at.

"I tried," I said.

And I had. It was the weirdest thing — like nothing I've encountered before or since. We already knew Holmes was a dichrome, making his mind a self-defending fortress. What we learned only with time was that his charisma extended beyond his own mind, plenty capable of swaying others. Holmes was so successful a criminal, we later learned, because he could make just about anyone like him. When he built his castle, he fired every worker after a few days or weeks — a tactic that obscured the castle's murderous design while also protecting his budget. He never paid men whose work he declared unsatisfactory, but more shockingly, none of them came back to shake him down or complain. That massive vault on the third floor, it turned out, had been installed by a bank, yet Holmes had paid nothing for it. He'd simply ignored the bills, but the expense of removing the thing prevented the bank from reclaiming it. He bought furnishings on credit and never paid for those, either. He bartered for land and property and never paid. Everyone was bamboozled by the man, who was always cordial, never argumentative. Even Ned, Julia Smythe's hapless ex, had inherited Holmes's old pharmacy across from the castle as a "parting gift" from Holmes ... only to learn that he'd also inherited Holmes's debt. Holmes didn't need to beg, borrow, or steal. He was the kind of man who could get people to give up freely what they held precious.

That's what he'd done with Minnie — and, perhaps, Emeline, Julia, and unknown others. With Minnie, we saw the effects live. I tried to talk her into leaving and failed. I tried to glamour her into leaving and failed. Dracula tried as well, also coming up short. We found the same walls within her as I'd found within Pitezel. The only difference was that in Minnie, those mental obstructions were made of opti- mism and faith rather than the fear that held Pitezel's secrets at bay.

Put simply, Holmes tended to brainwash those who came close to him — those he wished to collect and keep. He wasn't a vampire, but he was something else we learned about later, and able to corrupt minds. Something able to protect Minnie from our best attempts to free her to help herself.

She was sweet. And wealthy. Minnie owned land in Fort Worth valued at $30,000 in 1893 dollars — a sum that'd equate to nearly a million dollars today. What she owned was a deed, though, not cash. It should have been hard for Holmes to finagle *land* from anyone, but he got it easily from Minnie — just as, at several points, he convinced people near him to take out life insurance on themselves and name him as beneficiary. The deal with Minnie went easy as pie. Before the Chicago Fair even opened on May 1, Holmes somehow got her to deed her property to a man named Alexander Bond: his own alias. Holmes even served as notary. Not long after, he and Minnie used part of that money to rent a place in Lincoln Park, presenting themselves as husband and wife. This, despite the extortion, was fine with me. With Holmes spending more time away from the castle, I had more freedom to explore without him. I know being away irked him, but he had so much else to tend — women to extort, women to kill — that he could only spare so much energy watching the vampire in his midst.

Holmes came and went. He tended his pharmacy on the ground floor and of course he tended the hotel. I was pretty sure by then that the hotel itself was part of his plan, but for reasons I didn't yet understand, his personality somehow kept me from exploring much. He was strange about the basement, to which I couldn't find an entrance. He'd shut himself in his office or second-floor quarters, vanishing for long periods of time. Sometimes I'd swear I heard struggle. I'd hear his familiar, heavy-footed walk as he moved here and there within the hotel, but Holmes was always careful to move about during the afternoon when the sun was streaming in the west-facing windows — times I couldn't peek out and check on him. I had visions — dreams, blood, or fantasy, I don't know — in which I became sure that heavy-footed tread was hoisting a burden. I'd listen for his feet on the stairs, but he never went down. Sometimes he went near Edna's old room and sometimes I'd hear him near the bathroom. Then he'd retreat, never stepping outside or even downstairs. If he'd been doing something he shouldn't, how was he erasing the evidence? His quarters and office were clean; he made a point to leave the doors open as if to taunt me. If he was killing people, he was being covert. There were no bodies, no blood, no sounds indicating struggle. No heavy objects dragged out back, no screams, no nothing. Weeks passed that way. I convinced myself everything was ominous ... but fine.

Looking back, I think my judgment wasn't just faulty. It felt actively subverted. Sometimes I'd smell gas, and I've wondered since if Holmes, who used asphyxiation as one of his methods of murder, sent chemicals into my room to disorient me. I'm a vampire, so gas could never kill me. If Holmes was feeding it to me, however, it could have impaired me. I'd feel swimmy and trippy all day, then clear-headed at night when I left the building. Maybe I was being poisoned. In retrospect, both explanations for my tendency to "just keep gettin' on" (rather than acting against Holmes) feel flat and hollow. Both feel like an excuse — a story — that I tell myself today to assuage my guilt over failing to stop a monster. At the time, though, that's how it was. Holmes was nothing if not willful, nothing if not charming, nothing if not persuasive. Maybe I was gassed, maybe I was influenced by unseen things, or maybe Holmes had spellbound me the way he'd spellbound Minnie. Maybe I was just apathetic and lazy, willing to let innocents die if it meant keeping Holmes alive long enough to learn what I needed to claim that vial of blood. In the end, it made no difference. Those who died ended up just as dead.

On the night before the Columbian Exposition finally opened — April 30th of 1893 — a night finally came when Holmes left the hotel after sunset. He'd taken Minnie out, attempting to smooth her over. I'd heard them arguing in days previous, Minnie agitated through the agitation of her sister, Nannie. Every week or so Minnie would get a letter from Nannie, which she'd read for Holmes in a voice I could hear through several walls. The fact that Minnie read them to Holmes at all was testament to Holmes's power of persuasion, seeing as the letters accused him and tried to warn Minnie.

Nannie's letters made one thing clear: She thought Holmes was a con man and a charlatan. She thought he was taking advantage of Minnie's naiveté, which he was.

Holmes listened patiently to each letter, never speaking badly about Nannie's criticism of him, then soothed Minnie's concerns by explaining that Nannie was a good sister to worry. She was simply misinformed. Holmes's solution to the Nannie problem was simple: He invited Nannie to come stay with them, travel expenses paid, in their Lincoln Park home. He invited her to attend the World's Fair as his guest and promised to spend several days taking both women around to see its wonders. Nannie, I'd learned from last night's letter, wasn't too proud to be bought. She was coming, of course, and excited despite her earlier misgivings.

That night, Minnie wanted to celebrate. I heard Holmes murmur (wouldn't Minnie prefer celebrating away from the hotel during the day, so someone could watch the desk at night?) but Minnie was, for once, having none of it. They went out. Then I went out, too.

I'd explored the hotel before, but after weeks of being outfoxed by Holmes, who usually left me alone only during the day, I resolved this time to make my explorations worthwhile.

I started by exploring the first floor, looking for a stairway into the basement. I found nothing. I broke my way into the closed tinsmith shop, moved the bench, and opened the door to nowhere. It led, as things turned out, to nowhere. There were stairs, but they led into blank ceiling above and blank floor below. I tested both, found them solid or otherwise impassable. I then circled the building, looking for windows or recesses or coal chutes — anything at all indicating access to a basement. Again I came up empty.

"The hard way, then," I told myself.

I got a pad and a pencil, then snagged a measuring tape from Holmes's always-ajar office. I'd already been through his files and found nothing, convinced the office itself was a decoy and that Holmes's real affairs were chronicled elsewhere. The obvious office was kabuki, staged to present an image.

With tape in hand, I began to measure the rooms on the first floor. I then compared exterior measurements to interior ones, then subtracted to find the difference. Most of the walls were the expected thickness, and after an hour I started to wonder if I'd been imagining things. I was high on gas, perhaps; no wonder the passages felt twining and missing space like a funhouse — like a mad place with hidden chambers. But then I discovered something curious: When I compared the Wallace Avenue frontage of the building to the sum of the inside width of all the stores, there was a discrepancy of over twelve feet. Even accounting for unusually thick walls, there was still plenty of missing space: a ten-foot dead zone between the store and the saloon, as it turned out.

I spied the building from across the street. The simplest solution was to break through the walls and see what was behind them. But there was still a voice in my head warning me that no, I couldn't do that. I couldn't let Holmes know that I knew, or the game would be up.

What game? a second voice wondered. But my higher mind didn't even hear it.

In the end, I didn't answer my own question. I'd been living with Holmes in a state of curious hypnosis for what felt like forever, ignoring matters I should have attended and eschewing actions I could easily have taken. Why *hadn't* I killed Holmes, if I was so certain he was bad? Might as well ask why I never broke all his doors, bringing down the building if necessary to find its secrets. But more and more I had an answer, troubling as it was: *I didn't kill or disobey Holmes's intentions because something was stopping me.* Nothing mortal should have been able to stop me from doing as I wished ... but there I was, bound and gagged.

Dracula and I had locked Holmes into a nullspace between action and inaction, glamouring him into letting me stay but unable to glamour him into giving himself up. Holmes, on the other hand, had locked me into a similar nullspace. Through his magnetic force of will or something stronger, he'd made me stupid. Made me tentative. Made me resort to measuring and picking locks instead of destroying and killing, as I normally would have.

"I'll break it if I have to," I whispered to myself as I looked at the north wall of the saloon. "But so far, I don't have to."

I wasn't sure I believed myself. Every time I thought

about breaking something to expose Holmes, an invisible hand held me back.

For now, I had time. I had the night. Even without breaking anything, I knew I could play detective just fine.

It was time to delve deeper.

So I did.

THIRTEEN

SNOOPING

I went to the window. Looked out. There was what appeared to be a child in a trenchcoat on the street corner. The figure turned. It was Wyatt, the dwarf. I raised my hand. Wyatt took the signal, vanished around the next corner, and came back a few minutes later to throw me a high sign. I knew he'd gone to the club down the street and used their shiny new candlestick telephone to call the administration building inside the fair boundary, where all sorts of newfangled instruments — including Bell's telephone, reimagined — were set up for tomorrow's opening. It was the sign that our network of weirdoes had eyes on Holmes and Minnie far from the hotel, and I was therefore safe to proceed.

I re-entered the shop, eyeing the wall, wondering again what kept me from breaking it. I told myself: *Exposure. You're doing nothing because if you break it, it will expose you to Holmes.* I ignored the pushback that arose inside me — the sense screaming at me that Holmes had almost for-sure killed several people, and that letting the cat-and-mouse game between us continue was of no importance. If I broke the right things, I might find evidence I could take to the police. Dracula would renege on his offer of blood if that happened (I'd not yet discovered what happened to Emeline), but who cared? It was a small price to pay to rid the world of a criminal. Which, I kept having to tell myself, would be exactly what'd happen if I separated his head from his body.

Do it. Find the evidence you already know is there, I told myself. *Wait for him to come home, then kill him. Make him suffer, the way your core tells you he's made others suffer.*

But ... nothing. There was an invisible wall inside me. Invisible handcuffs binding me.

To the second floor, then.

I measured, scoped, measured again. Best I could tell, the dead space between the saloon and the shop on the first floor was exactly below the second-floor bathroom.

I opened the washroom door, preparing to enter. A woman came down the hallway holding a small basket filled with toiletries, a towel slung over her shoulder.

"I'm so sorry," she said, suddenly modest. It was as if, by seeing her intent to take a shower, I'd actually seen her naked.

"It's not a problem," I said, meeting her eyes, adding some glamour.

"It's not a problem," she repeated. Then she turned and went back the way she'd come.

I waited in case there were more. I'd heard people moving in the hotel all evening long, but the aural environment in that place was as strange as the physical one. I felt as if my ears were surrounded by funhouse mirrors, distorting my normally acute abilities. The woman just now was the first I'd seen of the humans in this place, but there had to be others — some, maybe, wondering what the strange young Frenchman had been doing for the better part of an hour now. I had no idea how many guests there were. Holmes kept shuffling them in daylight, churning our occupancy the way he'd churned through workers to build the place. To keep everyone guessing. To keep his secrets.

When no other humans arrived, I entered the bathroom. I felt stupid. Why had I come up here? The hidden chamber was below and did not seem to cut through the second floor. But I'd found no hidden doors down there, no way inside — even from the street. So what else was there? When lateral action failed, I'd decided to rise above.

I got to my hands and knees. I peeled back a corner of the bathroom rug and rapped on the floor, hearing how akin it was to a knock on a door. I waited again for curious humans but nobody stirred. There was a pall over the castle — always — and it made few people stir after dark.

The floor was hollow. Not joists-and-space hollow like you'd hear from any second-story floor, but the kind of hollow that betrays just a single panel of wood.

Heart pounding, I scratched back the rest of the rug like a dog digging in the yard, tossing it into the corner. My fingers ran tentative patterns over the wood, searching. Then I found it: a seam, a concealed latch. With effort I saw how to open the trapdoor, then lifted it up.

There was a hidden staircase through the bathroom floor.

I peered downward. The trapdoor opened sideways and wide, as accommodating as a farmhouse root cellar. With the door leaned against the modest-sized bathroom's sidewall, most of the floor was available for descent. I could walk down without bumping my head, and did. A few seconds later I was in a tighter space where I was required to turn in the other direction: a closet of sorts where, during open hours, I'd have heard the saloon on one side and the shop on the other. Ahead of me was what looked like a sealed-over portal: the go-nowhere door at the back of the tin shop, I assumed.

At the other end of the switchback was another set of stairs, this one decidedly more rickety. I could see exposed rock, more monoliths than brick. It was the foundation, surrounding access to the basement.

Not a crawlspace, as Holmes had said, but a full basement. The ceilings were over six feet high — tall enough to stand.

I walked forward, suddenly approach-avoidant. I needed to see what was down there, but couldn't. I was suddenly awash in terrible vibes and a reticence that gripped the back of me like a warding hand. For a while I wasn't sure I *could* move forward, even if I wanted. It was a stronger version of the hunch that kept me from breaking walls or attacking Holmes: a sense that *I'd just better not.*

I looked for a window, just to see the outside world one last time before descending. Of course there was none. I'd signaled to Wyatt, but all my wave told him was that I was snooping harder, knowing that Holmes wouldn't immediately return. Wyatt didn't know where I was right now, or about the trapdoor I'd found. He didn't know what I'd discovered. He wouldn't be able, unless he walked up to the second-floor bathroom, to find me.

And if the door above were to close? If the carpet were re-drawn over the hatch?

I pushed the thought from my mind. It was very, very, *very* hard to remember that I was a vampire. I didn't notice the feeling until it had me by the throat, and feeling it left me empty. For two millennium, I've been what I am. So what was I now, by this emotion? Did I feel like a human?

But no; I had no idea how to feel human. Mortal, though, like I might be killed at any moment? That, I could imagine. Weak? Helpless? I could imagine those, too.

There was a broken-away bit of stone on the floor ahead of the downward staircase. I picked it up. It was the size of a baseball, too large for my fist. I squeezed. The thing cracked easily, my hammer grip reducing it to dust.

See? You're still strong. If anything went wrong, you could just break out of here through the walls. You could break through the floors. And if it got bad enough? Brother, you know you can fly.

I tried to listen to my own litany. I had no idea why I couldn't truly hear it. There'd been a spell over me ever since I'd come to the castle, and right now its hands were around my throat. There was a glow from below, as if Holmes had rigged permanent gas lamps instead of relying on lanterns. It was firelight yellow, flickering in a draft. I could feel it like foreboding. I didn't want to go down there. As if Holmes was down there — only, not *Holmes*. Holmes, as an ordinary man, I could handle. What I feared was gut-level instinct, inaccessible to my higher mind. What I feared was something I couldn't see or hear or touch. Something I couldn't explain.

It was inside my head. Inside my soul. Something in this place that was not-man, not-vampire. No. This was something else.

I crept forward. Made myself go.

Down the final wooden staircase, holding onto a rickety bannister.

My feet trod bare earth. The ceiling — the first story's floor — was low here, just a few inches above my head. The cellar was wide and undivided, supported by occasional foundation posts sunken in artificial bedrock. Chicago ground is too close to the lake to be sure-footed; the fair's architects said it was like building on quicksand. Holmes had done his best, having workmen sink pillars in protruding columns of concrete. So far, it had worked. So far, his house of horrors remained standing.

The basement smelled. It wasn't just must, but something else. As I left the area around the staircase, the odor intensified. I pulled a handkerchief from my pocket and used it to cover my nose and mouth. There was something acrid nearby — a throat-irritating wash of chemical odor that inflamed my sinuses. Circulating now, I saw the origin: there was a pit filled with quicklime and loosely covered with boards to prevent falling in. It wouldn't do, to fall into quicklime. Slough your skin right off your body.

There was a furnace, full-fire. A massive one.

Wooden tables, stained so deeply I thought at first the wood was another color. The tables had restraints screwed to them: wrists and ankles. A drain in the floor was surrounded by another stain, impregnating the dirt. Where could the drain go? Merely to gravel, which had been soaked with ...

Oh, who was I kidding? I knew what it was soaked with.

My nostrils flared. Even with my brain on alert, the presence of all this blood — even dried — set my fangs on edge. I became aroused; I grew an erection. With my mind so alarmed, my body's reaction felt like a betrayal. I forced it back, still weak, still somehow compelled by a thing I couldn't see.

To one side, there was a pile of laundry.

Only: Not laundry. It was Edna Van Tassel. I knew by her clothing, her build, her jewelry. She was starting to decay, tossed there as if forgotten. Approaching, I scented something else chemical: a second pit filled with what had to be lye. Surely that was where Edna's body belonged, right? In the lye? Horrified, I walked closer. When I pulled boards off the pit, I saw why Edna hadn't been dragged there. The pit already had an occupant: a person of unknown gender, naked of both clothing and flesh. Little more than a skeleton, which ...

I stood. In the ceiling above Edna's corpse was a black box going nowhere. The ceiling was low enough for me to reach up and touch that black box's insides. Its walls were smooth, coated in something slippery. I sniffed: grease, possibly the kind used for oiling machines. The greased shaft extended upwards, dark but visible with vampire eyes. It stopped at the roof, meaning the shaft above pierced all four floors, connecting them like a spindle. I knew where we were on the floorplan, too. My internal compass told me that Edna hadn't gone far from her old room. If you mapped the second floor directly above us, we'd have been near her door, near the place where she said she'd heard Holmes dropping laundry.

I looked up. Not a laundry chute, after all. Holmes had architected a body chute into his plans, so he could drop them from above and dispose of them below.

I crossed the chamber of horrors again. Near the work-bench area with the two macabre tables (*dissection tables*, my mind recited) was a hanging skeleton — the kind you might find in a school room or college. Only, as bright white and wired together as its bones were, I knew the skeleton was real.

He was killing people, mostly women. Then he was bringing them down here, turning some to skeletons for sale. Others, I was willing to bet, he simply fired in the furnace — or, for all I knew, did something worse like eating their flesh. This wasn't a profit motive for Holmes — though, being a good businessman, he'd worked profit into it. No, this was psychosis. This was bloodlust. This, I thought as I took in the many gadgets and nuances Holmes had built into his mortuary, had been built for satisfaction. For his very own joy.

It made me wonder about the other oddities I'd noticed in the floorplan — the other spots where my gut portended hidden rooms. Now I knew about the bathroom staircase and the chute, but what else was lurking? What was the vault on the third floor for? Why were some of the interior rooms not just dim, but entirely light-tight? There were seals inside the vault, as well as hints of the same in other places. I began to wonder how many rooms would be airtight when closed. One daytime, I'd heard Holmes and Pitezel shouting but it hadn't turned out to be an argument. They'd been taking turns, screaming to ask if the other could hear them. It made me wonder: Were any of the rooms *sound*proof? I'd been able to hear both men, but I'm a vampire. To humans, wherever they'd been testing may have been soundproof enough.

You have to go to the police, I thought.

Then: *No. You have to end this yourself.*

But still I sat in the basement, knowing I needed to move but unable. Something anchored me. Something held me to the spot.

I thought of the gas lines I'd seen in one room, with the controls for those lines in another.

And I wondered how I'd been so stupid. How I'd never seen it before. I'd *suspected* plenty, but I'd done nothing at all. For my entire stay, I'd been in this place, fighting H. H. Holmes in a battle that was only of wills. I'd know the castle was strange. Hell, workers around town had *told* me it was strange. I knew there'd been disappearances. On my very first day, the freaks had told me rumor said Holmes abducted and murdered people.

So why had I done nothing? Why hadn't I stopped using my head to fight him, and started using my teeth instead?

Answer: Because I was just a visiting man from a foreign land. I was here to see the fair, not play vigilante.

But it was a lie. It was a half-truth. I've always avoided entanglement where I could, but I've never flinched from doing the right thing when my hand was forced. I'd turned a blind eye to Holmes. I'd let him do what he did right under my nose, and as far as I could tell there was no excuse for it.

I heard small feet above. A rough, quick patter where no feet should have been trodding in the late hour.

"Maurice?"

It was Wyatt. I climbed the stairs, only noting the absence of rotting stink once I was back in the sealed closet on the ground floor.

"*Maurice?*" He was just across the wall. In the saloon, I think. Holmes kept his business tenants' keys on a hook in his office, which he left open as a decoy distracting from his true purpose. I'd left the all three of the shops around this closet open, and Wyatt must have walked right in. I'd need to remember to re-close, or else I'd be caught.

Why are you worried about being caught?

It was a good question. I'd spent the past ten minutes too unnerved to be angry, but now that I was out of it my fury was growing. Holmes had killed at least three people, but I was willing to bet there'd been more. There were still unknown rooms right here in this hotel, and for all I knew there were captives tied up inside each of them.

So break through all the walls. Find what's hidden. Rescue whoever you can.

But my hands stayed at my sides. My feet refused to send me after Holmes, to wring his throat.

"Maurice!"

"I'm in here, Wyatt."

I heard him walking in confused circles, trying to find me.

"Inside the walls."

No response. Then: *"What?"*

"I'll explain later. What's going on?"

"It's Holmes," Wyatt said. "He dropped his lady friend off at their place, and is on his way here."

I looked up, toward the trapdoor into the bathroom. I had to get out of here, find Holmes, and rip his head from his body. Only ... I knew by now that I couldn't. Something was stopping me from going after Holmes, and it was time to stop ignoring what I knew in my gut.

What *was* Holmes? What had he done to me? Why, when I considered my options against him, did I feel so paralyzed?

There was only one person who might know. Only one person who'd kept that knowledge from me.

"Wait there and we'll walk to the midway together," I told Wyatt. "I have an asshole I need to visit."

FOURTEEN
NECROMANCY

I stared at Dracula. He stared back with theater in his eyes, as if he found this funny.

"This is serious," I said.

"I know it's serious."

"You lied to me."

"I didn't lie at all."

My eyes fixed on the vampire. He was such a dick. Never answered questions directly, always made me dig. Every time I talked to Dracula, I ended up on my knees. I hated it. He wasn't worth begging. Not in that stupid get-up of his, not with the put-on accent shouting *"I vant to suck your blood!"* and definitely not with his blathering about riding fashion's crest. Dealing with him made me dig my fingernails into the flesh of my palm. It made me want to punch him in the throat until his trachea collapsed.

"You told me Holmes was a dichrome," I said.

"He is."

"You let me believe he was *only* a dichrome."

Dracula seemed to consider this. Then he sighed, sat back in his chair, and put his powdered hands behind his head. He must have known I was at the end of my rope. Weeks of playing errand-boy to a fuckface will do that to anyone.

"What's on your mind, Maurice?" he asked.

Now that Holmes had returned to the hotel and I was miles away, my nerves had receded. Gone was that strange sense of fear and oppression. Gone was the force that bound my hands. I hadn't run to the police yet, but that was half the reason I was here: I suspected I *couldn't* go to the police just like I couldn't kill Holmes myself. After seeing the slaughterhouse in the hotel's basement — a hotel that had been designed for torture, killing, and disposal — I was ready to face what I'd been ignoring. Now I had proof, and wouldn't let myself walk away. Not if Dracula would just tell me what I was facing instead of blowing smoke. Not if he'd just give me the tools to do what I should have been able to do all along.

"'What's on my mind' is the vibe Holmes puts out," I snapped. "'What's on my mind' is the energy that keeps me from doing anything to stop him or stand in his way. He's killing people in there. I saw it just this evening. But every time I thought about ripping out his spine, I locked up. I know you know more than you're saying if you've been studying Holmes, so do me a favor and don't deny it. You could have gone into that building and found what I found, but I've noticed how being close to it causes you pain. That's why you asked me to do it instead, right? You should have been able to take care of Holmes without me — but my guess is, you can't hurt him. So you turned to me, hoping I'd be immune to the way he affects you. But I'm not immune. We're both in the same goddamn boat. So how about you tell me, *Eugene?* Tell me what boat we're in."

Dracula looked uncomfortable. The room was quiet. It

wasn't just us; Wyatt, Tatiana, and Koo Koo the Bird Girl were also in the sideshow tent, watching the vampires square off. They'd seen me run Dracula's errands before today, but they'd see it no longer. I was his superior in every way. By the rules of vampire conduct, he should have been kissing my ring. As he would be, from here on out.

A frown creased Dracula's face. At first I thought he might fight back out of pride, but in the end he was smart enough to know when he was beaten.

He sighed.

"Our best guess is that he's a necromancer," he said.

"You mean someone who fucks corpses?" Wyatt asked.

"That's a necrophiliac," I explained. "He said 'necromancer.' Like a ... like a *wizard*."

"Don't be an idiot," Dracula said. "Wizards don't exist."

"Just like fairies," said Wyatt.

"Fairies actually exist," I said.

"Werewolves, then."

"Save you some time, Wyatt," I told him. "Lots of mythical creatures exist. Thunderbirds, wendigos, incubi, succubi, you name it. Just not wizards. And do you want to tell them *why* wizards don't exist, *Eugene*?"

Dracula crossed his arms over his chest, annoyed by my repeated use of his name. He answered anyway.

"Wizards don't exist because they were invented by human fantasy. Specifically, a fantasy that humans can become like we are. Only they can't, because they're humans. They can't fly or see the future or accomplish anything by waving magic wands. They want to believe it *so bad,* though. Bad enough to sell a medicine wagon's worth of powders, if they promise new abilities. Some day, I'm telling you, I'm going to find a way to capitalize. That Stoker guy who wrote the book I told you about? When the vampire thing starts to fizzle, I've got a whole new series of books to pitch him on. They're about an 11-year-old boy who learns he's a wizard and goes to a wizard school to fight other wizards. Just an average human boy named Horace Whitterbottom the Third."

"That's a terrible name," Wyatt replied.

"Get on with it," I said.

"Holmes isn't a *wizard*." He drew the word out, sarcasm thick, wanting to be clear how little I understood of what he'd had years to assimilate. "'Being a wizard' is like 'being a mermaid.' 'Being a necromancer,' on the other hand, is like 'being a scientist.'"

After a pause, Wyatt said, "I don't have enough information to understand that analogy."

"Mermaids aren't real—" I said.

Koo Koo let out a cry of anguish.

"—but scientists are." I turned to Dracula. "You said, '*Our* best guess is he's a necromancer.' Who were you talking about?"

"Other vampires. It doesn't concern you."

"Where are those other vampires now?"

"Weren't you listening? *It doesn't concern you.*"

I turned to Tatiana. "That means they left his ass. They saw what a clown he'd become and left."

"If you must know," Dracula said, "my old friends didn't leave because of me. They left because of *him*."

"Because of Holmes?"

"Explain," said Tatiana, tired of this. "Both of you."

I sighed, realizing I was going to have to carry this conversation if it was to make any sense. I had holes in my knowledge, but anything was better than letting Dracula lead.

"Necromancy is a study," I told her. "It's an ancient art

involving communion with — and sometimes control over — the dead. It's something humans can learn, if they have the right teacher." I looked at Dracula, thinking of his absent friends. "And if that necromancy is strong enough, it's something vampires fear."

"Why?"

"Because the best of them can influence us. Push us around. Neutralize our threat, and make themselves safe."

"Sure sounds like wizardry to me," Wyatt said.

"Wizardry requires magic. Necromancy just requires crossing the mental barrier between life and death. In truth, there *is* no barrier. Life and death are fluid."

"They don't seem very fluid to me," said Tatiana. "Once you're dead, I figure you're dead."

Dracula answered. "If you're talking about the mortal plane, that's true. But there are other planes. What humans call 'ghosts' are nothing more than energy crossing planes."

I picked it up. "For vampires, life versus death isn't a straightforward thing. We see the area in between as gray, not black and white. But the fact that we understand it comes from experience, nothing more. Before we can be born as vampires, we have to die to our human lives. In almost all cases, that transformation is a slow one. It doesn't just happen in a snap. For days — sometimes as long as a week — a new vampire can be in a state of limbo between human and vampire, between alive and technically dead. During that time, new vampires can often still walk in the sun, but they see the world with vampire eyes. They hunger for blood, but can still survive on their human digestive systems. Having a foot in both worlds is just one way the boundary is flexible. Anyone who studies can learn to see it — and learn to control it, if they're knowledgeable and powerful enough."

"And?" Tatiana asked.

"Any human with some training in necromancy can learn to see the comings and goings of the dead. But only really, *really* accomplished human necromancers — I'm talking, trained the way warrior monks train — can actually learn to control the dead." I looked at Dracula. "Including us."

"And Holmes is a necromancer?" Tatiana asked. "One of the really good ones?"

"It's not clear." Dracula sighed. "I wasn't always alone here. I used to be part of a nest. But when Holmes came to town, it's like someone started rendering hog fat. We *smelled* him right away. It made everyone uneasy. The others started having problems sleeping, as if he was screwing up the energy in the air. So we sought him out. Tried to get close — kill him, drive him away; it didn't matter.. But ..."

"But you couldn't."

Dracula nodded. "When I get too close to him or that building, I get a bastard of a headache. The midway is just far enough that I don't usually catch his vibes, but as Tatiana told you, he visits often. I've had to leave before, just to protect my sanity."

Wyatt turned to me. "Maurice, you're staying in the castle. Do you get headaches?"

I answered as if my answer was a surprise even to me: "No, actually. I guess because I'm older and stronger. But I can't fight him. I couldn't bring myself to break locks or walls, even. Fortunately, I had no trouble snooping so long as I didn't cause damage. He's tried to make me leave, and I won't. It's limited."

Then I got it. Suddenly, I understood. I knew why had Dracula watched my approach from Europe. Why he'd summoned me right away once I arrived. Holmes affected me much less than he affected Dracula. I could be close; I could disobey; I could do just about anything but hurt him or call in the rangers. It wasn't like that for Dracula. He was young, just like his whole American nest must have been young. They'd be ... what ... one, two hundred years old at the very most? No wonder they'd feared him and no wonder they'd fled. A powerful necromancer would have affected them far more than a vampire of my years.

"You thought I'd be immune, didn't you?" I asked. "You thought I'd be able to walk right in there, find out what he was up to, and kill him without a problem."

Dracula's head bobbed. His body language had changed. He'd gone from posturing to surrender. From withholding to forthcoming. The cards were on the table now, for better or for worse. "We couldn't do anything, but I thought maybe you could. Holmes is a dichrome and a necromancer, but he's still only human. He bleeds when he's cut. He seems to age. He doesn't come out only at the full moon, or anything else."

I turned toward Dracula, trying to view him in a new light. I'd spent so long seeing him as a grandstanding buffoon that it was hard to believe he'd once been just one vampire of many, probably a junior member of his nest. Now the others were gone and he was alone. The persona of "Dracula" was a defense mechanism to be pitied, not a joke to be laughed at.

But yeah, I thought, *fuck that. I'm going to keep laughing at him anyway.*

I stood and paced, trying to think.

"He's a murderer," I said. Inside my mind, I kept seeing the bloodied dissection tables, the furnace, the lye pit, the bodies that used to be Edna Van Tassel and God knew who else. I kept thinking of the vault on the third floor. Of the other missing rooms, airtight, light-tight, and soundproof. He wasn't just killing his victims. He was locking them in. Terrifying them. Feeding on their pain and fear. Then he was gassing them to death while they screamed in the darkness, nobody able to hear or help them. "He's a monster, and he has to be stopped."

If only I could find a way.

"But I can't touch him," I said. "There's nothing I can do."

"No," Tatiana said. "But maybe I can."

FIFTEEN

NOT CAUGHT

"Tatiana," said Annabel.

Maurice's head bobbed.

"The bearded lady."

"Actually, Tatiana was the *painted* lady." He turned to look at her. "You know." He indicated the length of one arm using the other. "Tattoos?"

"How was 'the painted lady' supposed to help anyone against Holmes?"

"I'm getting to that."

"Why didn't you just call the police?"

"I told you," Maurice said. "I *couldn't* call the police. What Holmes did — without effort or maybe even conscious awareness — was like glamour to vampires. I couldn't have ratted him out to the police any more than you could tell the world about me."

Well, Annabel *had* told her husband about Maurice. Nobody else. She supposed that was close enough, and not worth a mention.

"If not you," she said, "how about Tatiana call the cops, or one of the other freaks?"

"Holmes was an upstanding citizen — a pillar of the community. Everyone loved him. Tatiana — or any of the others, for that matter — was a sideshow freak. People didn't look at tattoos then the way they do now, especially on women. She didn't have just one or two, you know. She was *covered* in them. No self-respecting policeman would take her seriously. If she went down to the precinct, they'd have arrested her first and asked questions later."

"She could have called, then."

"Phones weren't common in 1893."

"You know what I mean, Maurice," Annabel said, frustrated by what almost felt like an engineered no-win scenario. What, had someone walked around "the Holmes issue" and buttoned up every loose end? Surely there'd been a way. Murder was murder, even back then. She knew they'd eventually convicted and hanged Holmes. For well over 100 years, the case had been as dead and buried as Holmes himself, but thanks to Wikipedia Annabel knew how the intervening times had turned out. She kept wanting Maurice to say he'd done what history said he hadn't — for his story, here and now, to somehow erase the sad events that had followed. Knowing the story's truth as she did, the color Maurice added was more frustrating than intriguing to Annabel. Why hadn't they stopped him? It should have been so easy.

"I do," he said. He was looking at the ceiling again, lost in guilt. "But at the time, the plan we had in mind felt more likely to succeed. And it's not like we helped nothing. It's not like what we did didn't end up making the world just a tiny bit better. It just ... wasn't enough."

Annabel listened, reserving comment. He'd said, *It's not like we helped nothing.* But given that Holmes had gone right on killing throughout 1894, how could their stupid plan have helped a thing?

"The way we figured," Maurice went on, "Holmes had an exit plan. He had to, because so far he always had. He used people like pieces on a chess board. Even Pitezel. *Especially* Pitezel. Did you read about Pitezel? About a year after our *tête-à-tête*, Holmes got him to take out a life insurance policy on himself, presumably to fake his own death. He named Holmes as beneficiary. Holmes decided 'faking it' was overrated, so he killed him for real and burned his body to cover the trail."

Annabel tapped her pen. Maurice wasn't looking at her as he spoke — perhaps feeling the non-helpful, non-professional judgment she shouldn't have been feeling.

"If Holmes had an exit plan," Maurice went on, "he'd be too clever to be captured. He already had scapegoats lined up and a full bag of delaying tricks. He also knew his reputation in Chicago, and how easy it was to charm just about anyone he met. He knew CPD wouldn't barge in on the word of some freak or anonymous word called in via telephone — not without paying him a courtesy visit first. If we managed to sic the law on him, he'd charm the police who came, show them the safe parts of his building, then run off. Of course he would. He did that exact thing the next year, when a fraud charge finally caught up with him. Our only choice, at the time, was to snare him. Ideally, to kill him. Either way we needed incontrovertible proof — the kind that'd be obvious to everyone and not leave room for Holmes to wiggle away."

"But ..." Annabel was still trying to fit the last piece. "But *sending in the painted lady?*"

"Holmes liked her. She was young, pretty ... and, as anyone would assume from all those tattoos, psychologically damaged. He'd trust her, because he was a narcisist. He didn't think anyone was as smart or capable as he was — especially not a woman, especially not one he believed he'd 'chosen' as prey. If we sent Tatiana — not me, not Dracula, not a cop in disguise — he'd never suspect a thing. She could be our inside person in a way I couldn't. Holmes and I were locked in a standoff. He'd never try to hurt me just like I was unable to hurt him. Because of it, I'd never see his asphyxiation chambers. I'd never have seen the hidden stairs or the greased body chute or the basement if I hadn't weaseled my way in. But Tatiana? If we sent her in as a mole, she could see it all. She could *expose* it all."

Annabel considered making a comment (*"Guess she didn't expose enough, huh?"*) but bit her lip. She was personalizing the story, imagining her loved ones as Holmes's victims. But this was a story from long ago, and the here and now was supposed to be about Maurice ... not Annabel.

"You said Tatiana was strong," she said instead. "You said she was independent and didn't take anyone's crap. But you must have known that wasn't enough to keep her safe from a big man who used locked doors and gas to do his work, didn't you?"

In the space between her question and Maurice's answer, a thought flashed through Annabel's mind: Maybe Tatiana *hadn't* been safe. Maybe in the next chapter of this story, she died. Holmes was convicted for nine murders, but at one point confessed to 27. There may have been more. And who'd have missed one forgettable freak from Chicago's sidelines that history had failed to record?

"We weren't quite that naive," Maurice said. "I haven't yet told you the beauty part."

SIXTEEN
SHITFACED

Dawn was coming. Tatiana was nervous.

Dracula and I both told her not to worry, that only in the rarest of cases was the first day a problem. We were more concerned about ourselves. The night was almost over, and both of us were uncomfortably far from our homes, taking risks we shouldn't in the interest of saving time. Holmes, by then, had been murdering for a few years — if not the whole of his life. There wasn't really a rush, even in retrospect. But after I saw what I saw in his basement, everything *felt* like a rush. If we didn't get Tatiana in place soon, I felt as if our small window of opportunity would slip away.

"My hands are tingling," she said.

"That's the blood."

"My blood?"

I shook my head. "Your new vampire blood."

She was radiant. I wished I'd been able to read her, but only Dracula could. He'd turned her; I'd just sat and watched it happen. I had reservations about making because I saw it as a responsibility, but Dracula saw it as a kind of undead free love. Tatiana didn't want a daddy or a protector, and I'd have tried to be both. It was easier this way.

I wasn't exactly sure which blood she was feeling. Dracula's blood would feel new and inexperienced inside her, whereas the bit of Amadeus Macht's blood she'd sampled from that old capsule (psychic camouflage, to hide Dracula should Holmes turn out to be more than we imagined) would feel older and wiser. It was a subtlety I'd have been able to appreciate, but that any human would miss entirely. She was a naive user, high on vampire blood for the first time. There was no accounting for vintage. To Tatiana, both bloods would be an opium speedball, hightailing it for her cortex and adrenal glands.

"I feel drunk," she told us, "but otherwise not very different."

"The sun will feel different," I said.

"Because it'll kill me."

"I keep telling you. Not yet. You have *days* of daywalking left. That's why this is going to work. It's the *only* reason it will work."

Normally, brand-new vampires are walking liabilities. They don't really know what they are yet; they don't understand blood ties; they're barely stronger or faster than they were as humans. But for our purposes, the state of in-between came with advantages as well. Because Tatiana wasn't fully vampire, Holmes's necromancy wouldn't affect her much, if at all. It wouldn't hurt her to be around him in the way it hurt Dracula. Holmes would have no control over her that he wouldn't over a human — which meant that for at least a few days, she'd have better control around him than me. Tatiana would be able to kill Holmes if she needed to and found the means, and she'd have no problem blowing the whistle once she had proof. She'd be close to invulnerable, more likely to die from her vampire side's weaknesses (a stake, if not yet the sun) than a human one like knives or bullets. She could walk in the daylight and accompany Holmes wherever he wished to take her before "acquiring" her. What's more, even though she wouldn't yet be able to communicate directly with her maker, Dracula *would* be able to tap into her, seeing as her defenses wouldn't yet be strong enough to keep him out. He'd know where she was at all times. He'd know if she was in trouble, though it was still a bit of a question mark as to how we'd summon help since we couldn't fight Holmes ourselves. My bet was on the freaks, who we'd already briefed. I forget the name of our strongman, but he had a big waxed mustache and lifted trapezoidal weights while wearing a leopard skin. If Tatiana got in trouble, I was pretty sure I could get that guy running through walls to reach her.

It was the first time I'd seen the half-and-half state (some vampire and some human, but fully neither) as an advantage rather than a weakness.

Tatiana walked on, dazed and overwhelmed. Lost in all the thoughts not native to her head, by the look.

"I keep thinking of a man," she said. "A ruler. A vast, vast empire."

"Probably Charlemagne," I said.

"I don't know who that is."

"Amadeus Macht did," I said. Then I waved it away. "Don't let it confuse you. You have two vampires' blood in you right now to blur your signal. It won't always be like this."

I watched Tatiana, still seeming drunk. But that gave me an idea.

"This way," I said.

It was the evening before opening day, and the outside-the-fence crew had been up all night. Soon they'd make their big address and open the Columbian Exposition to the world. Until then, the few hundred thousand in waiting were determined to get their groove on.

I wanted to test Tatiana's transformation, and I had just the idea in mind.

We went to the Pabst tent, right beside where Buffalo Bill's Wild West show had set up camp just outside the gate, its ranks already open and overflowing. The Pabst team was ossified, just like most of those around them. I wasn't sure if they were supposed to be giving out free samples, but they were. It was just like when we'd come this way weeks ago and been given beers, only this was much more abundant.

At the tap, I asked the man for a sample. He handed me six beers. I couldn't even hold them all. I wrapped my thin arms around them as best I could, then found Dracula and Tatiana on the sidelines.

I shoved them into Dracula's chest. His fake count's metal tinkled against the bounty.

"What's all this?" he asked.

"An experiment."

"It looks like beer."

"*BEER!*" came a chorus of other voices. It was exactly the way, a hundred years later, that the barflies at Cheers would greet Norm.

I looked over. I saw the entire freak show approaching, already shitfaced. Apparently the Pabst party had been going on all night, and apparently the freaks had been some of the hardest-drinking among them. All had armfuls of beer like I had. Several shoved them at Dracula, having seen me do the same. Beers were dropped.

Yeast reeked from all the effluent as they spilled and broke.

"What am I supposed to do with all this?" Dracula asked.

I'd kept one in my hand. I opened it and gave it to Tatiana. To Dracula, I said, "Give them to her, one at a time."

Tatiana smirked, seeing this as a challenge.

"I can drink you under the table any time I want," she told me.

"I'll bet you can, but I'm not drinking. Only you. Only Tatiana."

"*ONLY TATIANA!*" called the drunk freaks. The Yucatan twins fell over, both at once. Nothing seemed to have tripped them. The others tried to shove PBR at her. She pushed them back, looked at me to see if I was serious, then downed it faster than any man.

"Satisfied?" she asked.

"Not even close." I nodded at Dracula, who gave her another.

Twelve beers later, the sky had begun to purple. Sunrise would happen quickly, but I needed to see the end of this test.

"Why are you trying to alcohol-poison her?" asked the spider child. Nobody knew its gender. Or its origin. Or possibly its species. We only knew that it kept climbing the uprights of the under-construction Ferris wheel, causing occasional mayhem.

"We're not trying to poison her," said the bearded lady. "We're trying to make her fun."

"I'm plenty fun," said Tatiana.

Five beers more, and Tatiana should have been barfing Tesla coils. Instead she simply looked bloated. In the coming light, I could see mist rising from her. The mist was good, just like her ability to remain upright was good. In simple but unhelpful terms, the mist meant she was venting. It's how vampires process excess intake, since we're mostly invulnerable. When we consume faster than our bodies can excrete, we just sort of slough the rest off. Anyone standing above Tatiana and breathing heavy that day would have ended up wasted.

"How do you feel?" I asked.

"Fine," she said. The word came out surprised, as it should have. Then she pointed at the other freaks, who seemed to have taken Tatiana's test as some sort of drinking challenge. They were a miserable heap, puking and crawling and moaning and nearly dead.

"Give her another."

Dracula did. "I don't see the point of this."

"Holmes might try to knock her out. He could use chloroform or something. I wanted to see if she was metabolizing like a vampire or a human."

"You said she'd be able to eat human food for a few days," Dracula said.

"She will. But alcohol is processed differently. It works on the nervous system in a way that food doesn't. I wanted to see if we could knock her out. But this is good. A ton of Pabst and she's not even tipsy. She should do fine if Holmes tries to dope her."

"Wait," said Tatiana, horrified. "Does this mean I can't get drunk anymore?"

"Hey. You were the one who said you'd always wanted to be a vampire."

Someone slapped me on the back very hard. If I wore dentures, they would have hit the dust. As it was, caught off-guard, I almost staggered to the ground.

"Who's a vampire? Vampires are pussies!"

It was Buffalo Bill Cody. He was chewing tobacco. Or cud. He smelled like the inside of a ferment tank and was holding a PBR in each hand.

"How about you, honey? You a vampire?"

"No," said Tatiana. It was half true. She was still half human.

"What about you two penis-biters?" he demanded of me and Dracula.

"No."

"Well, good. Because I hear there's one on the midway. Dresses like some sort of a fruit." He looked Dracula over, just now seeing the cape, the medal, the powdered skin, the tuxedo with cummerbund. Cody's face seemed to say, *Don't say nothin'. Let it go, ol' Bill.* The next time he talked, he talked only to me.

"Anyway. Can't be nothin' worse than the Injuns out on the prairie. Or the *coyotes.*" He said it ki-yotes. "You know what a lot of those people think?" He indicated the crowd around his Wild West show. "They think it's all jest fer fun. It ain't. I *did* all the stuff we talk about, all the stuff we do in the show. That's my home out there on the range, you know."

"My home is Transylvania," said Dracula.

Bill looked at him, then turned me so the two of us could talk alone. "I'm a *hero.* You know that?" He hiccuped, drunk as a cliche. Whatever he'd been chewing on leapt past his teeth like a tiny animal. "Real American hero, and don't you let nobody tell you no different. Same for Annie over there. You know why she learned to shoot so good? Rapists. You get a lot of rapists out west, so Annie learned to pick 'em off like a shootin' gallery. Some days, there'd be nine-ten rapists just come over her fence. When word got around she's a crack shot, they stopped comin'. *That's* how you make a name for yourself in the west."

"That's how I'd do it," Dracula interjected.

Bill looked at Dracula, then pulled us farther away.

"Listen, son," Bill told me. "I been watchin' you. Seein' you come through here, watching the lasso tricks—" Pronounced *las-ooo*. "—and doin' your thing. You're a leader, son. I respect that."

"You've been watching me?"

"Right now, I see you takin' care of that girl. Making sure she gets what she needs, 'cause she shore ain't gonna get it on her lonesome."

I wasn't sure what this meant. I also wasn't sure if he was kidding. Getting women wasted wasn't, traditionally, the same as taking care of them. But Bill was an unconventional sort, and also had the blood-to-intoxicant ratio of an embalmed cadaver.

"You wanna get your girl drunk, I say get her drunk."

This seemed to be a compliment. I said thank you.

"She wants to yak, you let her yak."

"I'm not going to yak," said Tatiana.

"That's the spirit. Anyway. I could use a guy like you. A leader. You interested in a job, son?"

"Um ..." I spied the horizon. The sunrise was dangerously close. We'd be lucky to get back to Dracula's tent in time, and zero chance I'd make it back to my room at the hotel. Great. A full day in the company of Bella Lugosi. Not that I knew Bella Lugosi at the time.

"Well. Anyway." Bill clapped me on the back again. "You think about it. My name's Bob. Find me if you need me."

"I thought your name was Bill."

"Bill, Bob ... who gives a shit?" Then without preamble,

he reached into his cheek with a hooked finger and raked something away as if it'd offended him. He threw something onto the ground and stomped on it. It stuck to the bottom of his boot. "WHAT THE FUCK IS THIS CRAZY TRAIN?" he demanded.

"Excuse me?"

But Wyatt had figured it out. He was kneeling at Buffalo Bill's feet, holding up the boot with the crap stuck to it, sniffing like a dog. Bill saw him and shook him away like a pest. But too late; Wyatt had his answer.

"It's called gum," he said. "Juicy Fruit."

"Is it food? Is it tobaccky?" Bill kept spitting and hooking his finger inside his cheek as it to rid himself of the last of it. "Fuck a walrus, son   what the living shit *is* that mess?"

"You chew it until it loses its flavor," I explained. "Then you're supposed to throw it out."

"So I ain't supposed to swallow it."

"Not as far as I know."

Wyatt, despite the stomping, had managed to pick the gum off of Bill's boot. He was staring at it now: a crusty blob of dirt-colored snot. There were free samples of that somewhere too, and yet Wyatt looked like he might recycle what Bill had finished.

Bill looked down. His expression was one of a near miss.

"Well then," he said. "That's *exactly* why I need you. Tell me what's juicy and what's not. You think about it."

"I will, sir."

Buffalo Bill ambled off.

"So," Tatiana said, looking at me in the relative silence that followed. "Am I drunk yet?"

"No," I told her. "And that means you're ready."

I woke to find Dracula's arm draped across me inside the extremely cramped travel trunk Dracula used as a bed. Just my luck: "sleeping in cramped spaces" was the one way in which Dracula wasn't a total poseur. If it was bad for one vampire, it was terrible for two. Normally, I slept in wide-open rooms whenever I could, ideally on a bed with my wife. It was only the Tatiana errand that had gotten me stuck here, needing to cohabitate.

Strangely, flinging Dracula's arm away and attempting to extricate myself from that shitty little trunk made me miss Celeste. I resolved to send her a telegram before Western Union closed for the night. This wasn't like the time I spent in Austin in the 1980s, when one of my individualist fugues had broken the two of us apart for a while. This was a matter of time, money, social life, and convenience. We hadn't actually left France yet; that happened later, in the '20s. This was just a trip across the pond and back, even though it took months for me to return. We still had friends and commitments in Europe, so Celeste had stayed. Blood ties bridged the gap for us a little, but not enough. Waking to find Dracula's 1890s version of Drakkar Noir in my nostrils was a far cry from Celeste's delicate scent.

Dracula yawned, sitting up behind me. His demeanor was just a little sleazy, as if we'd spent the night fucking.

"Morning," he said.

"It's evening."

"Figure of speech."

Except that it wasn't. It was merely inaccurate. He might as well have pointed to the ceiling and said "floor."

I walked away from him, annoyed. He rose to follow like a lover seeking attention.

"Sleep well?"

"Fine."

"Want to get breakfast?"

"I'll grab someone when I leave." Which would be in, like, two hours ago.

"Something better. The fair is open, and we all have free passes. I know a place that serves crepes."

My nose wrinkled. Crepes or no crepes, French or not French, I haven't liked human food for a very long time.

"No thanks."

But I was having trouble paying attention to Dracula. The way the freaks' quarters were situated, we weren't inside the actual midway but were instead just beyond it. It was strange to think that the massive exposition the world had been hearing so much about — that Raphael and I had been planning to investigate and potentially cause mayhem at almost a year ago — was finally here. I could hear thousands upon thousands of people walking past not far away, along with tons of chatter. The live and populated fairgrounds was brand new to me (7pm was the best I could do for an "opening gong"), but the people I heard excitedly passing had been walking the grounds all day. They'd had all of daylight to explore and be excited. Even without Tatiana and Holmes, I felt somehow behind.

That made me think of Raphael Michaud and the mayhem we'd intended for me to cause here, to ruffle American feathers and uphold French pride. I guess that was out the window, seeing as I had a baby vampire to protect and a murderer to catch. It was curious: I'd been away from Michaud for months now, in a new land with new influences, and I felt nothing like the man who'd come to America with ill intent. If anything, other than Celeste's absence, I'd acclimated. It occurred to me that America wasn't so bad. Chicago, despite its filth and industry, wasn't so bad. I could live here. And Michaud? Maybe it hadn't been such a good idea to reconcile with him, wine feud or no wine feud. He was like a succubus, pushing my mind into a worse version of myself when I was near him. The Maurice I was now felt much more native. Chasing killers and hanging with freaks — that was the life for me.

"Are you leaving?" he asked.

"Soon."

He yawned. It didn't matter if there was a serial killer on our agenda; he wanted more shut-eye. "I'm too tired."

"Stay, then. I need to run an errand anyway."

"Eating, you mean."

"That, but I also want to send a telegram."

"To whom?"

It was easier to answer than to point out it was none of his business. "Celeste."

"Your wife?"

"Yes, my wife."

"Aren't you her *maker?*"

"Yes."

He seemed to consider pointing out the blood ties issue, but wisely decided to keep his mouth shut. Dracula didn't have a wife. He only had one-night stands. He didn't know how the little things counted. Yes, Celeste could buy flowers for herself. Yes, she could hear from me through our shared blood. That didn't mean gestures weren't meaningful — a way of reaching out from so far abroad just to say, *I'm thinking of you.*

"We should wake Tatiana," I said.

And by "we," I sort of meant "me." I'd gotten along well enough with Dracula last night, but I'd been drunk with the horrid things I'd found in Holmes's basement. I knew I needed his help, long-term, to keep Holmes glamoured, and last night had made him feel like a comrade. But now, with my mind focused and further from the shock of it all, he was annoying all over again.

Camel Girl was walking by on her backward-bending knees. She heard me and said, "Tatiana's not sleeping. She's been gone all day."

I dropped the glass I'd been holding. It was empty. Good thing I hadn't been drinking a vampire's version of a Bloody Mary.

"*What?*"

"She said she was going to the hotel." Camel Girl shrugged. I think her real name was Denise, but she preferred to stay in character. No point in letting the freak show exploit you if you could simply embrace it yourself and ride the wave. "I thought you already knew?"

I looked at Dracula, knowing he'd be as concerned as I

was. He wasn't. He was laying down to sleep again. "Just ten more minutes," he said.

I ran. The streets, particularly around the fair, were clotted with people. I couldn't move like a vampire; I couldn't blur past them like I wanted. Dracula talked a good game about just being a vampire out in the open, but his audience believed it was still part of the show. If they saw a real vampire and knew it wasn't a gag, they'd come after me with torches and pitchforks.

So I went like a human, far too slow. It was three miles to the castle from the midway, and without my usual speed the fastest I could get there would be fifteen minutes or so. Even then I'd look to outsiders like an Olympian sprinter.

I ran, headlong, into a man who looked a little like Albert Einstein. But it was decades too early for Einstein. Turned out, it was Mark Twain.

"Sorry," I said.

"It's no problem, young man." With all the air of a casual meeting, he adjusted his vest and poked at the chain on his pocket watch. He was wearing an all white suit like a cotton magnate. Possibly a pimp. I should have run on, but doing so suddenly felt unfathomably rude.

Twain went on, seeing my temporary decision to stick around.

He stuck out a hand. "I'm Sam Clemens."

His real name. I got it. I was in a hurry. But now he had his hands on his hips, blocking my way. He held a cigar, puffing it amiably. It was disarming. Who stopped to chat up a kid who'd nearly mowed him down? Still, I stayed, feeling seconds tick. The foot traffic had us hemmed in, especially after I'd ceased my rush and stopped, allowing it to happen. Now, I'd have to push him down to get by.

Clemens — Twain — puffed his stogie.

"Tell me," he said. "You look like a fellow with an interesting story. I'm somewhat of a *collector* of stories!"

This was all very interesting. I knew Twain, of course. Tom Sawyer and Huck Finn were mainstays even in Europe. But dammit, I had to go. I might even have been a little starstruck if I didn't feel like a life hung in the balance.

"I'm sorry," I said. "I really need to be going."

Twain grabbed me by the shoulder, physically restraining me in a way that might make a more alpha man strike him.

"Now hang on a second, young man. The lives we lead are composed of moments. Some, looking back, will turn out to have been more intriguing than others, but *all* are precious. Maybe this ... *engagement* ... you're so eager to rush off to is of the utmost importance, but — and you may call me presumptuous if you choose; Lord knows I've been called far worse — I would wager the chances are excellent that it's not."

He grabbed my other shoulder, now holding both, so he could assess me like an adult assesses a growing child after not seeing them for a long time. He had intense little eyes. With all his bushy white hair (head, eyebrows, mustache, all wild and trying to escape), it looked as if they were studying me through a cloud.

"Now *you* sir," he said, "*definitely* have a tale to tell. Having known you for the lengthy engagement we've had, that's something of which I'm positive. It doesn't matter that you're real instead of fictional; that's not something I'd hold against you. Take my latest book, hitting the stores of your local sundries shop perhaps as early as next year. The protagonist, with the given name of David Wilson, makes a misunderstood remark upon entering town and is thereafter thought of as a pudd'nhead. A simple event, but one that defines him. What defines you ..." He paused dramatically, waiting for me to fill in the blank.

"It's Maurice. But I really need to get g—"

This delighted him. *"Maurice!* I knew a mime once named Maurice. Terrible conversationalist. Tragic ending. He was pulling on an invisible rope and fell into an invisible box, where he suffocated." Twain removed his hat and bowed his head.

"I can see something in you. Something fathoms deep and acres fantastical," he said, now studying me, a bit less farcical and a bit more serious. I recalled Buffalo Bill Cody saying he'd noticed me and fancied me a leader, just by the look of me in a crowd. I'd never noticed before, but in America I must have stood out — some sort of perma-glamour, radiating casually through my pores. "I know we just met, but a storyteller knows a story and my boy ... I just *know* I want to write a book about you. So tell me, son. What's *your* story?"

I exhaled, then spoke:

"I'm a 1900-year-old vampire who came here from France to sabotage the Expo, but got sidetracked when I found dead women decaying in the basement of my hotel. Now another vampire, a dwarf, a pair of bald twins, a girl with four legs and a man with no legs, and a lot of people with excess body hair need my help to rescue a girl completely covered in ink who drank two people's blood last night before getting shitfaced on Pabst Blue Ribbon and Juicy Fruit."

Twain let go of my shoulders. He stepped back. He blinked.

"Perhaps a book about my travels following the equator instead," he said.

"That's a good idea. You could call it *'Following the Equator.'*"

"A bit too on the nose, don't you think?"

"Your call, Mr. Clemens," I said, finally spotting my opening to pass. The hotel wasn't far. I could see it in the distance. "I wish you the best of luck."

EIGHTEEN

GONE

I ARRIVED at the front desk out of breath. Of course, I wasn't *actually* out of breath. When you run the 440 in less than a second, springing through a crowd at sub-mach speeds isn't much more strenuous than reading a book. Something in me (adrenaline, or fear that something horrible was already done) had turned on all the same physiological circuits they would in a rushing human. It was for the best. It made Minnie, who'd been doing a crossword at the castle's front desk, sit up and pay attention.

"Mr. Toussant! Are you all right?"

"Tatiana. Have you seen Tatiana?"

"I'm sorry. I don't believe I know a 'Tatiana.'"

"Slight. Yea tall." I held a hand at her approximate height.

Minnie frowned, thinking.

"Covered entirely in ink drawings?"

Her round face lit. "Oh! Yes. That poor girl. Tragic."

"What the fuck happened to her?"

Minnie looked dumbstruck. Her hair was practically blown back by the force of my rudeness and profanity.

I tried again. "I mean, whatever happened in my absence?"

My outburst had been so out of character for the year, the decorum of the day, and Minnie's sweet demeanor in general that her brain simply erased it. She answered my newest question as if nothing was out of the ordinary.

"Oh! Nothing in your absence, Mr. Toussant. I was referring to that nice young lady's backstory. Her past."

"What of it?"

"She told me what occurred. About her accident."

"Accident?"

"Nearly died in a printing press explosion, don't you know." She lowered her voice. "Poor girl. She'll never find a husband as dear as my Henry."

"Henry ... ?" Then I realized she meant Holmes. "You two got *married?*"

"Well, don't tell anyone, but we're betrothed in *name* already — and in *fact* soon. Our home on the park would only rent to a married couple, so we lied." She giggled like a schoolgirl.

"You have to get away, Minnie. I mean it."

"Oh, I agree. I'm only here because of the fair. Henry is working in the second-floor bathroom ... although, come to think of it, I haven't seen him for quite some time. He just needed me to cover the desk for a little while. It's good that you already have a room, because Henry told me we only have female rooms left."

I let the idea of "female rooms" go. Minnie wasn't going to win any Mensa awards, and not just because Mensa wasn't a thing yet.

"I didn't mean you need to get away from the front desk of this hotel," I told her. "I mean you need to get away from ... from Henry."

Watching the confusion on her face broke my heart. This was the first time I'd seen her since discovering the corpses, and right now all I could imagine was Minnie at the bottom of the body chute, Minnie in the pit of lye or quick-lime, Minnie hung from a hook as a clean and articulated skeleton, all prepped for sale to the local medical school.

"Away from my Henry?" she said. "Whatsoever for?"

"Yes," said a voice. "Whatsoever for?"

I looked up. Holmes stood in the doorway. He stepped closer.

"Mr. Toussant," he said. "My favorite long-term tenant. Out after dark, I see."

"I like the dark. Small bathrooms, basements ... even a light-tight vault will do."

Holmes's eyebrows peaked, but only a little. We'd been playing this game for months, even though now was the first time I knew for sure what he was rather than merely suspecting. He was a murderer; I *knew* he was a murderer; Holmes *knew that I knew* he was a murderer. He under-stood the detente between us as well as I did. He couldn't move against me or throw me out because of the fragile glamour I'd crafted with Dracula. I couldn't move against him because of his dichrome nature and his necromancy. We were two steers with locked horns, unable to engage beyond the fixing of furious eyes.

Holmes's manner snapped in an instant. He'd been an angry monster, but suddenly he was Mr. Charming again. I'd seen it before. It didn't strike me as something a sane man would be able to do.

"Anyway," Holmes said, brushing his hands briskly together. "All's well and tidy. You'll be pleased to know the plumbing is once again functional. If anyone asks, Minnie dear, please tell our guests that the central bathroom on the second floor may again be used. Just in time for evening bathing."

Then Holmes looked at me again. I wanted him to leave. Minnie was stupidly easy to glamour. I'd done it in the past. The problem was that Holmes, somehow, was always able to glamour her right back. His charm was superhuman. This time, though, I'd make it so he'd have no opportunity to reverse what I'd done. I'd tell her to run — run like the wind! I'd tell her to board a train, change her name, and never look back. Good luck to him, if he wanted to glamour her back after that. He'd have to find her first.

But Holmes stayed where he was: at Minnie's side with one hand on her shoulder, as if he knew what I was thinking.

The door behind me burst open. It was Dracula. He stuck out like a nail with a too-tall head, but we'd done this song and dance before. Keeping Holmes glamoured was like flossing: We had to do it over and over if we wanted it to stick. That meant we'd paved our way, making even his absurd get-ups known to the staff. I'd told Holmes's rotating cadre of desk girls that Dracula was a performer and soft in the head. The first part was true. The second part ... well, that was also true.

Dracula, like me, seemed out of breath. For him, it may have been a real thing. He wasn't as old or strong or fast as me.

"Thank God," he said. "They were almost out of crepes."

He tried to hand me something that his clenched fist had turned into an ejaculating penis made of dough.

"Here's yours," he said. "You owe me ten cents."

"Eugene," I said, ignoring the crepe and trying to draw his attention to Holmes.

"Dracula," he corrected.

I elbowed him. He followed my gaze, seeing the standoff.

"Maybe we should go up to my rooms," I suggested.

Dracula nodded.

We left them alone, but my heart kept reaching out to Minnie. Despite my attempts at detachment, I was emotionally entangled in the question of Julia Smythe, who I'd promised to find for Mamie before I'd sent her packing — no need to leave one more young, sad woman alone in Chicago for Holmes to find. Mamie sent me regular letters, a few photos of Julia for my hunt, and even a handful of sketches. Mamie was equal parts forlorn and optimistic — forlorn because Julia was gone, optimistic because she had faith I didn't have that I'd bring her back. I knew in the pit of my stomach that it wouldn't happen. Julia was dead, as was Edna Van Tassel, as was Dracula's girl Emeline. I think Dracula knew, but we didn't discuss it. Officially, I was Dracula's proxy; I was still going to find Emeline — possibly alive — in exchange for that vial of blood. Unofficially, I think we both knew the score. It was easier to pretend we didn't.

Now, atop all the other heaviness, I had Minnie to worry about. And possibly her sister Nannie, who I'd just remembered was staying with them. Fresh meat in the making, both of them.

"What is it?" Dracula asked as we walked the hallway. He was still holding the mutilated crepe. I think he'd forgotten it was there. It hung in his grip like a dishrag.

"It's Minnie," I said. In the half-minute it took for us to walk the corridor, I told him what she'd told me.

"It's okay. We'll get him first. She'll be okay. That's why Tatiana is here."

Of course, that remained to be seen. All I knew of Tatiana was that she'd entered the hotel. But I also knew Holmes had spent a good part of the day "in the bathroom," which meant in his slaughterhouse basement. He already had three projects going down there. Why not kill off the newest renter and make it four?

We reached my room. We went inside. I noticed fresh scratch marks around the doorknob, invisible to most but clear with a vampire's attention to detail.

"He's been here," I said.

"Wrong," said someone else.

It was Tatiana. I couldn't help myself; I crossed the room to hug her.

"You're cold," she said.

"You're not," I replied. I put a hand to her forehead like a parent checking for fever. "Your change is going slowly. That's good. It gives us time. How do you feel?"

"Like everything is sharper," she said.

"Are you hungry?"

"Just for food." Then her head snapped toward Dracula and she told him, "Yes. I hear you fine."

I met her eyes.

"I can't have a conversation with him yet, I don't think," she told me. "But I can hear him if his mind is loud, and I think ..."

She squinted, scrunching her face with effort. Dracula grabbed his head with both hands.

"Yes," Tatiana finished. "It seems he can hear me as well."

"You don't need to shout," Dracula said.

She smirked at me. It seemed she'd known that, and she'd shouted with her mind just to irk him.

"Why are you in my rooms?"

"Mine have no windows." She pointed to the windows I'd covered, from which she'd removed all the blankets. "I've come and gone a few times. Went to the fair, figuring I should enjoy the sun while I'm still able. Holmes was gone in the morning, off at his other place. I used that time to explore the places you told me." She shivered, and I knew she'd seen something I'd rather she hadn't — one more reason she was supposed to wait until dark to come here, so we could protect her. "But the rest of the time, I needed a place to be. I didn't particularly want him to try killing me before we had a chance to speak and I wasn't sure I could wake Dracula while he was sleeping, even with a loud shout like this one."

She did it again. Dracula grabbed his head and said, "STOP THAT."

Another smirk. "So I stayed here, in your room, by the open window."

"How did you know which room was mine?"

"Minnie told me. She's very kind."

"Have you met Holmes?"

"Of course. He has a crush on me, remember? I told him I'm through with the sideshow. Enough gawking for me! I asked for his help booking a train out of town five days hence."

I didn't ask why. I understood, even without blood ties. Tatiana was the opposite of Minnie: whip smart, probably the most intelligent person in the room even with all my experience. I'd told her that her transformation to fully vampire would take a few days, so her request to book a train ticket set our timeline in stone. Five days from now, she'd be mostly if not fully vampire, and our little game between her and Holmes would be over. But on the other hand, if Holmes knew she was leaving in five days, he'd have all the incentive in the world to do whatever he intended before then. And not just incentive: a built-in alibi. The booker at the train station would surely remember a tattooed woman buying a ticket away from Chicago, but nobody would know if she ever got on the actual train. Her little gambit had baited the hook for Holmes with a perfect little time window. He'd act now, or he'd never get a chance for the woman he'd spent months pining for.

"That was dangerous," I said.

"But you admire it."

I reluctantly nodded.

"Doing this at all was dangerous," Tatiana went on, her tone businesslike. "If he's going to try and kill me, let him do it while my human side is still of value."

"And before his necromancy prevents you from acting against him, too," I added.

"And that."

"Do you think he knows?"

"Knows what?"

"That we're ... how would you say it? 'In cahoots'?"

I'd considered that. Only, no, that's not the right word. I'd *sweated* it. Our little plan would fall apart if Holmes thought Tatiana was visiting on anything other than her own volition. If he found out he'd protect his secrets more than usual, hang around and always be over her shoulder, then kill her the first chance he saw — no loopholes exposed. In the hour and a half I'd laid awake inside that cramped little trunk around noonday, I'd pored over all the loose ends and decided our tracks were sufficiently covered. I wouldn't have been willing to bank on it, though, and that's why it calmed me to know we'd get a chance to talk and plan with Tatiana before she headed into the lion's den.

Little did I know she'd take independence to a new level, deciding to go off without us.

"I think we're okay," I said. "I asked for you at the desk, but I asked Minnie, before Holmes showed up. Unless Holmes specifically asks her about you and me, I think she'll be too distracted by the fair to even remember we know each other. He knows Dracula works the freak show, but we set up our glamour so that Holmes tolerates me in his space but forgets Dracula entirely." I turned my attention to Dracula. "By now, I'm sure he doesn't even know you came, let alone that you talked to me downstairs. I've been around the freak show some, but never when Holmes was there, looking for Tatiana." Back to her again. "Tatiana. Can you think of anything you've done or said that might indicate you know me, or are here for any other reason than as a waystation before you leave the city?"

She thought, then shook her head. "I've been thinking and figuring all day. If you don't think he made the connection when you were downstairs just now, we're clean."

We stood in silence. There were hundreds upon hundreds of people walking by outside now that the fair had opened. According to what I'd spied through Minnie's hands at the front desk, the hotel was fully booked — even considering those "female only" rooms Holmes was renting.

"Now what?" Dracula asked.

"Now we wait."

"For what?"

I didn't want to say it. Fortunately, Tatiana didn't care.

"For him to kill me," she said.

NINETEEN
WAITING

But of course, Holmes didn't.

To stay safe, we decided Dracula shouldn't come to the hotel until the whole thing with Tatiana was over. We topped off Holmes's glamour, knowing it'd hold for a week at least, then sent Dracula packing. He couldn't stay close anyway; being around Holmes for too long caused him pain. Holmes knew of no connection between me and Tatiana, so we took pains not to interact or even cross paths while in the hotel. Instead we set a regular schedule of check-ins, wherein every few hours during the night she'd sneak away and I'd sneak away, and we'd compare notes at an out-of-sight bar down the street. If we'd had phones, Dracula could have connected us and made things safer: him at the midway listening to Tatiana's blood and peering through her eyes, then alerting me if she ever needed help. As it was, neither the hotel nor the freak show had a phone. We had to find another way to open communication.

The solution grossed me out. Dracula and I bit each other and drank each other's blood, knowing it'd give us a temporary connection. Intimacy with this buffoon was the last thing I wanted, but Tatiana's life might depend on our ability to talk quickly. Even so, it was cumbersome. We had to play the he-said, she-said game with Dracula in the middle.

The first night passed.

The second night passed.

In the middle of the third day, I startled awake and ran to my window so agitated that I almost ripped the blanket away for an impromptu suntan. I was suddenly sure Tatiana was in trouble; I'd seen it in Dracula's blood. In that paranoid vision, I imagined she was just beyond the window, in the middle of the street, and Holmes was sticking a knife between her ribs.

But just as my hand clasped fabric, my more sensible mind started to think. *Wait. He just dragged her outside in the middle of the day with all those people around? Killed her in front of everyone?* On one hand, it was a boon: We wouldn't need evidence if Holmes did something so public. Regardless, ripping away the blanket would do nothing. I couldn't run out and save her if my vision was true. I'd be ash before my feet touched the ground.

I held the blanket's edge, blinking in the darkness, waiting for that wave of panic to pass. Then I realized: What I'd seen wasn't real. Dracula was dreaming, and his blood had sucked me into his dream. I mentally yelled to wake him up and stop the vision, then felt pain as he woke and banged his head on the top of his sleeping trunk. Inside my mind, I heard a voice say, *You asshole.*

That night, nothing. Tatiana met me at our usual haunt: a working-class bar called Double Dog where Tatiana, wearing sufficient clothing to hide her tattoos, could pass for a welder chick.

"He knows something," she said.

"He doesn't know." I'd been stalking Holmes much more closely than usual, even venturing out in daytime so long as I could stick to shadow. Vampires would be excellent ninjas. Our speed and dexterity can, with practice, make our movements invisible. Our strength lets us do things that humans can only do in movies, like pressing ourselves into corners of high ceilings. Our sight and hearing are acute enough to see from great distances and hear through just about anything — including Holmes's otherwise soundproof vault.

Watching Holmes told me he suspected nothing. On the contrary: the fair, his extortion project with Minnie's land, Nannie's visit, and various other schemes kept him too busy to look over his shoulder. He wasn't even spending much time at the hotel, despite his full house of young, attractive guests. The night before, after making sure Holmes was far from returning, I'd returned to his basement of horrors. This time, though, only shadows of the old terror remained. There were still those wooden dissection tables, still the pits of lye and quicklime, still the crematorium furnace, still the dark stains everywhere indicating a bath of blood. But Edna's body was gone from beneath the chute, the corpse was gone from the pit, and the showroom skeleton was no longer in place. The last one — or possibly two — I was pretty sure I could explain. Once before dawn, I'd seen Holmes meet with a man I later identified as Myron George Chappell, known in certain circles as an articulator and broker of skeletons for medical research. He must have gotten a pretty penny for Holmes's skeleton or two, because that night Holmes treated Minnie and her sister to dinner on the town at a rather expensive restaurant called The Four Winds.

Beside me at the bar of the Double Dog, Tatiana kept

squirming. Part of it was her blossoming vampire nature, I knew. Just like a tethered mustang, this baby girl was harboring a growing need to find open country and *run*. She'd spent her pre-vampire days playing human, giving short shrift to her new abilities. It must have been like living inside a box.

"We're running out of time," she said.

I didn't tell her we had plenty of time. We didn't. Three days in and Tatiana only had one full evening left after this one. But even if she'd bumped back her train ride to allow Holmes more time to pursue her, it'd solve nothing. She was at least halfway through her transformation, her skin growing cooler and her eyes growing paler, more crisp around the iris. She moved too fast on accident now, not knowing how to contain her new strength and speed. Her sun sensitivity was growing — I'd watched her return from the fair earlier that afternoon, noting a sunburn on her previously unburnable skin. Worst of all, the closer we let Tatiana come to full vampiredom, the more danger she'd be in. She'd soon no longer be immune to Holmes's necromancy and find herself unable to act against him. She'd no longer be able to go into the sun, giving away our secret. Holmes knew I was a vampire; I was sure of it. Even if the top level of his mind didn't realize, his deeper levels did. You couldn't kill a vampire the way Holmes usually killed, but we're simple enough to dispose of if you approach by daylight or with a wooden stake in hand. Especially if we were bound by necromancy, unable to fight back.

"He's too busy with other things to obsess over you," I said. "You're going to have to be more aggressive if you want him to go after you before time runs out."

"I already have half my skin showing. Should I walk around naked?"

I shrugged.

"I was kidding."

"Maybe we should call this off," I said.

Tatiana shook her head. "Mamie sends me letters too, Maurice. I know you want to catch him for Dracula — for that vial of blood he promised you. But I owe this to Mamie, and Mamie alone. Her words are full of heartbreak. I don't know if she loved Julia or just liked her plenty. In the end, it doesn't matter. I know Holmes killed her. I can feel it in my core. Just like we all know what happened to Dracula's Emeline and God knows how many others. I'll be as 'aggressive' as I need to be. If I have to fuck him, I'll do it."

I'd considered it. I won't lie. I hadn't pitched the idea, but it'd crossed my mind. The field of abnormal psychology wasn't robust back then and the notion of serial killers was nonexistent, but I'd trafficked in enough minds to guess that Holmes's lust for killing went hand-in-hand with lusts of a more bodily nature. Killing — controlling, really, right on into oblivion — got him off. There was no better way to shortcut that process than to dangle meat before his hungry lips.

"I don't know if that's necessary," I told her.

"Bullshit. I may not share your blood, Maurice Toussant, but I can read the lie in your eyes."

We parted. She went back to the hotel, possibly to offer herself to Holmes as a way of forcing his hand, forcing him to try and kill her at the exact time we could arrange for the law to catch him in the act. That part (the only part that really mattered, in fact) had only bothered me in an academic way at first. Now it bothered me like a punch. From the beginning, our little scheme against Holmes had involved Tatiana dying. She'd be gassed; she'd be stabbed; she'd be poisoned; she'd be gutted like a fish. Her new vampire nature should protect her, but we always knew it was a gamble — Tatiana most of all. That's why I'd been so worried that first evening, realizing she'd gone alone and without our knowledge. It's why I was worried as I walked back to the castle now, feeling that formerly hypothetical situation suddenly close at hand.

But before Tatiana could make her move, something else happened first.

We arrived back at the hotel, separately, one taking care to avoid the other. But once in our rooms, Dracula connected our findings from his station at the fairgrounds:

A new girl at the castle's front desk told them that Minnie's mother had telegraphed twice.

Both Minnie and Nannie were missing, and Holmes had moved back into the castle without them.

TWENTY
BLINKED OUT

THERE WASN'T MUCH I could do. At great risk — seeing as Holmes was suddenly back among us, right there in the murder castle — I managed to get back into the basement for a peek, but found no new bodies. I checked the chute from top and bottom, having discovered its entrance behind wallpapered panels on the third and second floors. Nothing there, either, and I even leaned over the ledge, peering toward the dirt floor far below. The vault door was wide open, and even pressing my ear against all the too-thick walls in the place — the location of hidden suffocation chambers, most of which I'd found ways to open during the clock-ticking days as Tatiana matured — revealed nothing. Knowing Holmes might find me, I opened all those rooms and chambers just in case Minnie was dead inside. But there was nothing.

Daytime came. There was only a day and a half left until Tatiana's supposed train ride, and no more than that before she turned undead all the way. I kept up with my search for as long as I could, forcing myself to admit that Minnie wasn't inside the castle. I'd have to cross open streets to find her, and by then the sun was shining. So with great agitation, I rested.

Sleep came uneasily.

I dreamed of Holmes becoming a literal monster — a great, rotting thing with black eyes and antlers, not just burning the flesh from his victims but cutting it away and eating it instead. I woke with the feeling that some kind of intelligence, somewhere, was trying to tell me something. Even after the dream ended and I'd peeked out to confirm that it was dark, the dream stayed with me. Reluctantly, I found myself having to admit: *I was afraid of Holmes.* He was human and I was vampire, and I knew he couldn't hurt me. But as much as fearing for any of the women he'd chased, I realized I feared for myself. To look into Holmes's eyes was to look into a great and echoing nothingness. He was an empty tomb, an ancient thing wearing the cloak of a man.

Shaken, I checked the clock. I reached out to Dracula for news, but he too was just waking up. He asked me, in the nonverbal way of shared blood, if I'd had a quiet sleep. I read between the lines, knowing his question wasn't idle chat. He'd spent his day tossing and turning as well. Perhaps because our time was almost up and neither of us could shake the feeling that a trap was closing around us. Perhaps because of something more.

It was almost time for me to meet Tatiana at the Double Dog. We had planning to do. Whatever needed to be done, we'd need to do it tonight, or make plans for Tatiana to do it the next day while I slept. She was running out of time for a fluid seduction — the kind of time people began counting in hours. It had to begin now or the window would close. If, by tomorrow night, she'd gotten nowhere with Holmes, we'd have to call it off. She'd have to vanish. I'd try to talk to the police, knowing I'd come up tongue-tied. I'd talk to anyone. Anything to put a stop to him.

I sat at the bar at the Double Dog, nodding to the bartender. He brought me mead as always; I drank it for show as always despite it tasting like piss. Only after it was gone did I think to look at the clock again, but when I did, I saw that time had gotten away from me. It was later than I'd realized, and Tatiana was nowhere to be found.

I didn't want to take the time to mess with contacting Dracula through blood. Ever since that terrible dream, I'd felt less like a detective on the trail of a criminal and more like prey trying to outwit an unseen gang of predators. The dark is my home, but for the hour I'd been awake tonight it'd felt like an enemy. There were specters over both shoulders, amassing from the front and rear. My scalp prickled. It wasn't even Holmes that was the problem — at least not the Holmes I knew. I felt like there were a hundred of him. That if I stayed still for too long, they might surround me.

So I left the Dog. Went out back. Climbed the exhaust pipe for the place's oven, concerned only with the smell of burning flesh when its heat melted my skin. I didn't wait to heal. Once high enough, I leapt to the roof of the building across the street, then to the adjacent one, then across the street again. I couldn't run below or humans would see me. But up here, like a gargoyle on leathery wings, I was invisible.

By the time I reached the midway gate, I was too uneasy to fuss with the admission line. I leapt the tall fence beside the freak show tent, not caring who might see.

Dracula intercepted me before I could speak. For once, he was dressed like a person, not a joke. For once his face was intelligent, not dull and void.

"I lost Tatiana," he said.

"What?"

"You heard me. I can't feel her anymore. I can't see through her eyes or access any of her senses. I could, until ten minutes ago. Until—"

I lost focus. Ten minutes ago, I'd been at the Double Dog. Ten minutes ago, I'd felt so oppressed by shadows, I'd run here instead of using blood just to get away. The feeling was gone now, in the bright evening lights of the fair. Gone like Tatiana was gone.

"Did he kill her?"

Dracula shook his head. His hair was still slicked back and oiled, but coming apart to fly like loose shoelaces. "I don't think so. I've been trying to stay awake and pay attention, but I must have dozed off. I know she made contact — *real* contact."

"Did she … ?"

"I don't think she had to. I caught a whiff of her thoughts, not just her senses. She's still too new to keep thoughts inside. Something she saw or discovered must have convinced her that Holmes did indeed kill Minnie and her sister. I know she went to their Lincoln Park home, so maybe she saw something there. I tried to stay awake and watch, Maurice. Really I did. But it's the sun lately. This hot, groggy May *sun!* It makes my bones heavy. I can't—"

I held up a hand. "I know. It's fine." I'd felt it too. When the sun was high, investigating even with the blinds drawn was impossible. It was like trying to run a marathon under the cloak of morphine. "Just tell me what you *do* know."

"The thought I overheard from her," Dracula told me, "was about Holmes and Minnie. She felt sure Minnie was gone — where, I couldn't say. And she thought, 'Now that he's done with Minnie, he'll be eager for someone else.' She wasn't afraid when she thought that, Maurice. The girl is brave."

I knew that much, too. "Go on."

"From what I saw and what I dug from her memories of things I was asleep through and missed, I think all she had to do was to wag her hips in front of him. He no longer had a paramour, so he latched right on and took her bait. He wanted to ... Well, you know. But she cut him off. She said, 'Take me to the fair like a lady.' Implied right behind that was an unspoken word: '... *first.*' He knew what she meant. Treat her well today, sleep with her tonight. I was in and out when they came here by hired cab, then as they walked around for a while. She said she wished the Wheel was finished. She said she wanted to fly."

I swallowed a lump in my throat. I don't know why, but Dracula's recount of Tatiana's day with Holmes didn't sound like a report. It sounded like a tribute. Perhaps a eulogy. I heard, *She said she wanted to fly.* It made my heart hurt, sure such an innocent thought could only have been punished by death.

"Did they go back to the hotel?"

"That's the thing," Dracula said. "I'm not sure. After the sun went down, I was able to wake fully and pay more attention. After that, I watched them like a hawk. They walked the court of honor. They admired the architecture. They gazed up at the Statue of the Republic at the head of the pool, Holmes holding her hand only after Tatiana reached for it. He was, by all accounts, a perfect gentleman. She had a guidebook and a map; I could see her looking at it. She claimed to have a list of exhibits she wanted to see. Holmes thought that was funny: a performer, who'd had early access to the entire exhibition grounds for months, had a *list?* The way he said it, her interest was adorable. She was as wide-eyed and spellbound as any other fairgoer after all — tough-girl persona be damned."

"So? What happened?"

"Holmes said that if she had a list, he had one too. He rattled off a few exhibits; I don't remember which ones. A lot of artifacts, like of ancient cultures. History. Anthropology. She asked if he wouldn't rather see the science exhibits, but Holmes said his work gave him enough science and medicine and anatomy. I remember that specifically: *anatomy*. It made me think of how you described his lair in the basement. How he wasn't just killing his victims. He was dissecting them."

"Get on with it," I said, feeling seconds tick away. I understood his agitation: He'd been the watchman tasked with keeping prisoners in their cells, and yet he'd let a prison break happen right beneath his nose. But in the moment his guilt didn't matter, and neither did his need to explain himself. All that mattered was that Tatiana had gone radio-silent — something that should only have been possible if Holmes had erased her from existence.

"They argued," Dracula went on. "*Fake*-argued, more like playing. I felt her mind wanting to get to business, and business wasn't at the fair. She needed him to take her back to the hotel. Lock her in a room and do what he wished. She trusted us to get her out before anything bad happened; that much I know. We don't need to *tell* the police anything, Maurice. I know we can't *tell* them. But we can *call* them and tell them where to look. You know that's the plan."

I felt like slapping him. None of what he said was helping. I understood that he was panicked, encountering perhaps the first truly mortal situation of his afterlife. I could be calm; I'd had centuries of murder and mayhem to dull my senses. But no matter how much I tried to be patient with Dracula, I couldn't shake the feeling that a new clock was ticking and its seconds were running out. I knew we could call the police. I knew necromancy would seal our mouths when they arrived. I knew the plan, goddammit, just like Tatiana and Dracula knew the plan. He was just flapping lips, getting us nowhere. What I needed to know wasn't what Tatiana wanted of Holmes or what Holmes planned to do. We knew both of those things. What I needed now, more than anything, was simple: *to know what had actually happened.*

"*Dammit,* Eugene! Get to the point!"

He took a breath, making an effort at calm. "Okay. Yes." Another breath. "Last I saw, they were heading away from the pool, heading north. But I also know that Tatiana was flirting with him, and flirting *hard.* Trying to get him to lose interest in the fair, see. She'd gotten him to give her a day out instead staying in and fondling, but now that it was dark, she meant to get him back so we could do our part. So I was watching. Very, *very* carefully. I was just about to contact you and let you know the time was at hand. We needed to be close, because there was still Ben Pitezel to consider, and Pitezel might need dealing with. But just as they were trying to decide where to go — to one of the fair exhibits each of them wanted, or back to the hotel — she just ..."

"She just what?"

Dracula shook his head.

"She just ... blinked out, like she'd never been there in the first place."

Now that Dracula had gotten to the point, I didn't know what to make of it. I stood there blank-faced, letting more of those precious seconds tick away.

"She ... *'blinked out'*?"

He nodded. "One moment I had perfect access to her blood. The next, nothing."

"How?"

His face pinched. "How the hell should I know?"

He was agitated. So, *so* agitated. I let my eyes sigh closed, then open, then patted the air for calm. "It's fine. Let's just try to think." I didn't want to say the next thing, but it was the most obvious: "How sure are you that he didn't kill her?"

He swallowed, accepting my plea for calm, and nodded with his answer. "Very. At least not then — that's not what caused the blackout, I mean. They were together near the pool, like I said. Near the statue. Have you been that way?"

I shook my head. This was the fair's first open evening, and I hadn't exactly had time to sightsee.

"It's packed. *Packed.* I've heard people say there's something like a quarter million people here, maybe more. They weren't even inside a building. They were right out in the open, in the thick of a crowd that'd be a pickpockets dream. Arm to arm. Shoulder to shoulder. And brightly lit — Edison electric, not gas, powered by dynamos. There was no way he'd do it there. No way he *could*."

I had to agree. So what, then?

"Okay. When did this happen?"

Dracula looked at a clock standing opposite us atop a black iron post. "Ten minutes ago. Fifteen at most."

I stuffed down my irritation. Fifteen minutes was an eternity. He should have called out to me right away. That's *why* we'd gone through the repugnant ritual of sharing blood in the first place. I could guess why he'd waited; it was because he felt guilty for his lapse of concentration and thought he could fix it — or find her again — before reaching out. It didn't matter. What was done was done.

I pointed to something barely seen ahead. "Is that the Statue of the Republic there? The told one with the swords?"

"Right. That's where it happened."

"Did you go there right away?"

His lips pursed.

Motherfucker. Cowardly, stupid motherfucker.

"Dammit, Eugene!"

"*I was waiting for you!*"

I told myself: *What's done is done. Focus on what you can change, not what you can't.*

"Did you see where they were headed?"

"I told you. They were trying to decide where to go when I lost contact."

"So you don't know. You don't know if they stayed at the fair or headed for the gate."

"No. I don't."

Well, thanks to your quarter-hour delay, I thought, *they could be halfway to the hotel by now ... or lost in a crowd the size of a city.*

I sighed, fighting the urge to lash out. "We'll just have to look. I'm faster and have better vision, so I'll search the fair. You go back to the hotel. And *run,* you bastard. I don't care who sees you; you run like Satan himself is chasing!"

"But *you* know the hotel," he whined. "It's not just Holmes that gives me headaches. So much of his soul is in that castle. The building itself is crippling to me, whereas you're already used to its—"

I grabbed him and shook him hard enough to rattle teeth. *"I don't give a fuck about your headaches! If you don't get to that building and scour every last goddamn hole and trapdoor I told you about, I'll kill you myself!"*

I let go violently, leaving him to stagger. He stared at me with wide eyes.

"Go," I said. "I've got the fair."

And I did. I surged down the long east/west arm of the midway plaisance, toward the first set of uniform white buildings, ornate in architecture and capped at the same height. Past the dynamo-lit walkways with their throngs of well-dressed pedestrians, along the canals with their ornate electrically powered boats. The Statue of the Republic was near the southeast end. The magnificent, domed administration building stood at the far end. The pool there was oblong, parallel to the massive pier. It was supposed to reflect Columbus's long journey across the ocean to the New World. Or something.

But there: *Nothing.* Of course I found nothing.

My mind ran a million miles a minute. Searching for Holmes and Tatiana in the massive crowd wasn't just like searching for a needle in a haystack. It was like doing so without knowing that there was a needle, fearing that the needle was dead and decaying somewhere in quicklime. My eyes hyper-sensitized, driven by fury and panic. My heartbeat became the metronome counting seconds. I began to see them everywhere, all my hunches just tricks of sight. If I saw them, it meant she was living. If I saw even Holmes — knowing there was nowhere here to do his killing — it meant she was probably alive. But what if they'd fled? What if they'd already made the hotel, but Dracula wasn't in time?

His mentality came to me. It was less a voice and more like a hunch with personality. My mind, used to blood ties, translated Dracula's thought as if we were on opposite ends of a Bell telephone:

I'm here. I'm at the front door.

After that, Dracula's thoughts spilled like mercury as he rushed through the building, sparing no speed. I could feel Dracula's ego stepping out of the way, trying to give me a direct line to his eyes. I could feel his regret. His worry. His sense of having done wrong. And he had; even trying to be kind to Dracula, I knew he had. Not just today, but yesterday, a week ago, two months ago. He'd involved me and I'd involved Tatiana. Julia had already been gone when I'd arrived and so had Emeline. My presence hadn't helped anyone. All I'd done, the whole time, was to stand by and watch disappearances happen. I hated Dracula for that. If he'd given me a task I could handle, I'd have been glad. But he hadn't. He'd given me a foe I could only observe, never counter. He'd put me outside a cage, then made me watch while the lion was fed its dinner.

That's when I realized how much of the guilt was mine. I wasn't just angry at Dracula. I was angry at me, too.

And scared. So, so scared.

He's just a man. And Tatiana? She asked to be there. She knew the risk. They'll catch him, somehow. They'll stop him, somehow. Even then, I knew he'd be stopped. Forensics didn't exist, but you couldn't do what Holmes did forever without leaving traces. And so, on the heels of that thought, I had another: *It's not your responsibility.* But I knew what I was doing, thinking that. I was trying to distance myself. I was trying to give up already, so that when the inevitable happened, I wouldn't feel so bad.

She's a vampire. He can't just gas her. He can't just knife her. But it was a small comfort. Vampires couldn't defy Holmes. He controlled the dead, and in order to control the dead you couldn't be entirely ignorant of it. What did that dismissive part of me think would happen, if Holmes locked Tatiana in a room and she didn't suffocate? Did I think he'd just let her go? Of course not. He'd take it as a challenge — no, no … a *delightful* challenge. For Holmes, controlling women was his drug. What was better than striving for a new level of control?

When Tatiana didn't die, Holmes would burn her. Bind her. If she broke the bindings, he'd chase her. If the sun was out, she'd catch fire. If Holmes know our lore, he'd use silver. If he knew our lore, he'd put a stake through her. And what, pray tell, would Tatiana be able to do to stop him if he tried any of it? She had her feet to run away, but that was it. Thanks to Holmes's power over my kind, she wouldn't even have her teeth to use against him.

I felt Dracula cede control so I could step inside his head. I peeked out through his eyes, but only for a moment. I didn't want his eyes; I needed my own. I threw it back at him, shutting my mind to all but the brightest bulletins. *Tell me if you find her,* I said. *One way or another.*

I focused on the crowd at the fairgrounds. There were far, far too many people for me to see any two of them, or even to use my abilities to give chase. Even if I knew where they were, I couldn't rush to find them. Even the tops of the grand white buildings were barred to me. They'd see me, up there in the light.

Nothing, I heard Dracula's blood say again. *They're not here. They're not here and I can't find them!*

I sent him mental pictures of the castle's tricks and secrets: every concealed latch, every trap door. From what I'd sampled of Dracula's mind, I knew he was a sloppy sort: easily influenced, weak-willed, hideously disorganized. He had strength for one so young; I'd give him that. And his mind — if he'd drop the stupid Transylvanian act — wasn't bad in itself. But right now I couldn't help feeling that he'd miss things if I didn't remind him of the careful files laid out inside my own tidy mind. My talent with blood ties made it easy for me to recover all those details and send them, but I wasn't sure Dracula was getting all the nuance. He just wasn't as good at it as I was. Some vampires are like that with blood ties. They can barely share the minds of their own makers, let alone strangers like me.

Now, paying attention as my own efforts failed to bear fruit, I held each of my own delicate memories in careful mental fingers and showed Dracula each one.

Did you check the 3rd floor chute? Here's how it opens. Did you try the vault? If it's closed, here's where Holmes keeps the combination. Did you try the asphyxiation chamber beside Holmes's office? There's no marked door; it seems just to be a fat spot in the floorplan between two rooms. You'll have to find it by the peephole behind the map on the office wall.

I climbed atop the engineering building to focus as my

mind went inward. Staying low, nobody below would see me. Between Dracula's nudges, I peered over the edge and scanned the crowd. From up here I could see just how immense the grounds were and how crowded they'd become on this opening night. My stomach sank. I began to hope Dracula would find her, even dead, because at least then we'd know. We were all sure Minnie Williams and her sister were dead, but they hadn't turned up at either of Holmes's residences. Precedent told us that Tatiana could just disappear, if Holmes wanted her to. That — after all the secrets and guilt I was already holding — would be a bridge too far. Even at my age, it would thrust a spear through my gut.

I pushed into Dracula, fist-deep like stuffing a turkey. I could tell the intrusion hurt him but I didn't care. *Find her. Find her! Alive or dead, we have find her!*

Then, deep into his memories as I was, I saw something new.

I found a rogue memory inside Dracula's mind: not his; Tatiana's. Something she'd seen, maybe something she'd even deliberately sent him. Tatiana was new — not even a vampire yet — and Dracula's talent with blood ties was abysmal. I couldn't see the memory well. It'd been distorted by Tatiana's mind, then ill-received by Dracula's. Peering closer, I started to think there might even be another layer, as if the memory didn't even originate with Tatiana. But if so, how could that be? She was just a baby. It was surprising that she could even talk to Dracula, let alone see the blood memories of anyone else.

It was all a mishmash. I began to think I was seeing psychosis for the first time in centuries: a memory so twisted and twined that it might have been three or four memories together. The kind of thing that happens with repression.

With deliberate guile. With things long, long forgotten — and intentionally so.

But whose? How? And why now?

In the memory of a memory of a memory, I saw a large book made of yellowed parchment. An ancient book. Then a hand — a woman's hand — holding something much more modern. In that hand was a printed map. Tatiana's hand? I wasn't sure. In that part of the memory, I could see walking feet below the map, as if others were passing close by. I could hear chatter and the press of bodies. If not for the intertwined vision of the old book, I'd have assumed I was seeing today, here, at the fair.

Then I saw Holmes's face. Smiling. Then the map again. Two fingers scanning the map, a man's and a woman's now. Together two hands turned the map over to find a long list of all the fair exhibits, rendered in tiny type.

I saw a building.

Then another building, far in the past.

All the memories collided, making a mess.

Then it was like a door slamming. Dracula's conscious mind was front and center, seeming to stare me in the face. The ball of blood recollections was gone as if it'd never been there.

What are you doing? I heard Dracula ask.

I thought of the book. Of the fingers pointing at fair exhibits on a map.

Nothing, I said.

And that's exactly what we found, as the World's Columbian Exhibition roared through its first night — as Dracula scoured the castle before returning to scour the grounds with me, the two of us spiraling out in twin circles:

Nothing.

We found nothing at all.

Dracula blinked awake. We were at the murder castle at the end of the following day, this time in my room, the blankets on the windows opaque and intact. On one hand I'd felt strange, returning to the scene of Holmes's crimes once the sun rose and forced us indoors. On the other hand, it was the perfect place to go. There was more darkness at the castle than at the fairgrounds, and Holmes couldn't harm either of us thanks to his glamour. I figured that if Holmes was going to turn up anywhere — if he hadn't simply boarded a train with Tatiana and left Chicago for good — this would be where he'd stop. And of course I wasn't going to sleep in Dracula's trunk again if I could help it. Come Hell or high water.

When Dracula's eyes opened, he found me staring into them. I could see around the drape's edges that the sun was still high and deadly.

"Holy shit," Dracula said, sitting up and scooting away from me as if I were a snake on his legs. When I didn't break my stare, he said it again: "Holy *shit,* you scared me! What's going on, Maurice? Why are you just sitting there staring at me? You're kind of freaking me out."

"Why are you like this?" I asked.

"What do you mean?"

"I've never met a vampire like you. You parade around in your ridiculous get-up. You use a fake pop-culture name. You brandish your fangs in public and affect an accent to tell everyone who and what you are."

"It's part of my act."

"You have an *act*," I added. "Vampires are supposed to be creatures of darkness and mystery. I can't think of a single one who's taken to the public eye — such an obnoxious version of the public eye — as you. Who was your maker? How did you become the way you are? Why weren't you taught our ways?"

Across from me, Dracula seemed to be struggling between offense and the desire for redemption. He knew he'd screwed up. If he hadn't known that last night (which he abundantly had), he'd be feeling it right now from his dreams. I wasn't staring at him because I found him attractive. I'd been staring because staring helped me focus. If I'd shoved my mind down his throat last night when I'd found that ball of confusing memories (the book, the fingers on a fair map), delving into his dreams just now had made that feel like child's play. I was suddenly very interested in Dracula, as we took this hiatus from our search for Tatiana and Holmes. My instincts told me to be interested. Some way and somehow, my questions for Dracula mattered.

In his dreams, I'd seen a dark shape looming over him. Dark like a child sees an abusive and domineering father.

He chose offense, as I'd thought he might.

"Who the hell are you to tell me how to act?" he

demanded. Then, a twist of his features. "Were you ... Were you *spying on my dreams?*"

I ignored him. Now was not the time for bullshit or posturing. Holmes and Tatiana had been missing for well over twelve hours, and by my estimation Tatiana couldn't have more than 24 hours left. After that, if she was still alive, she'd be a vampire. Holmes, as a necromancer, would see the way she stopped acting like a human flirt (or a human ballbuster, depending on whose switches had flipped) and begin deferring to whatever he did and said. My age and strength made me immune to Holmes's lesser demands, and even Dracula was old enough to merely get a headache. Tatiana, on the other hand, would probably just do whatever he said. It'd be a new kind of torture for Holmes to use — a kind, I suspected, that he'd rather enjoy. *Put your hand on that hot stove, dear,* I imagined him telling Tatiana. Then, while she screamed: *Now, hold it there forever.*

"Who is the man that looms so large inside your mind? The one who frightened you, and made you run?"

"I didn't run anywhere."

"Who traumatized you? Who arrested your development, and made you into the joke you are today?"

He stood. "Oh, fuck off, Maurice."

"Who did he kill? Who did you watch him slaughter? And the blood, Eugene. What of the *blood?*"

He went for the door.

"Going somewhere?"

"I don't have to take this from you."

"You gave me your blood. You *let* me do this to you."

"Assuming you had some decency," Dracula countered. "My dreams are private! My memories are private!"

He went for the door again. I rushed to it first, putting myself between him and the exit.

"Where will you go? It's daytime."

"To another room. To the 'asphyxiation chamber' for all I care. Anywhere that you aren't."

"You're covering something. Only ... are you? Because there's one thing I can't work out above all the rest. I didn't want to exchange blood with you. I hate it. It's as if you're in every pore — as if I couldn't wash the shit of you off my skin even with a thousand baths. My talent for blood ties is strong. You know it is. That means I don't even know how long your ... *pollution* ... will stay inside me. I don't want it; do you understand? I never did. I only agreed to swap blood because you were so insistent. *Why* did you insist I take your blood, Eugene?"

"We needed a connection," he told me. "If we were to send Tatiana after Holmes, you and I needed a way to talk across distance."

"Why?"

"Because I couldn't stay close to Holmes. I couldn't stay at the hotel. If he took her there, I needed a way to let you know if something happened and—"

"I could have exchanged blood with her instead of you," I interrupted, my manner intense but still calm. "We could have cut you out of the middle. We've already established that the time delay — waiting for you to hear from her and then let me know — was costly. Ten minutes too costly, at least."

He dodged the accusation. "You wouldn't have wanted to swap blood with Tatiana."

"I didn't want to swap blood with *you.*"

"She's a woman. It would have been like cheating on your wife."

"She's brand new. Her blood would have metabolized in half a day. If I was cheating with her, it'd be a one night stand. With you, it's like I'm suffering through a months-long affair."

"Nobody forced you."

"*You* forced me."

He seemed prepared to argue, but knew there'd be no point. I was right. Even before shoving my face into Dracula's sleeping mind for the past four hours, I knew I was right.

"I think you feel guilty about something. Something you hide very deep inside. I can see it in you. It appears to me as a black trunk. I've seen the same black trunk inside Celeste's mind. Only, there's one difference. Your trunk? It has a key."

Dracula tried to push past. I barred his way.

"I think that whatever you're hiding — whatever fucked you up and made you the laughable asshole you are — it's something you *wanted* me to find. You're like a cheating spouse subconsciously leaving clues, just begging to get caught."

"Bullshit!"

"You didn't call me when Tatiana blinked off. Instead, you tried to cover it up."

"I was in shock."

"Do you actually want to find her alive, Eugene? Or do you want to keep trying to protect your cowardly ass instead?"

"*Of course I want to find her!*"

He'd shouted it. Enough to startle the other guests in the murder hotel, if they'd been around. I didn't think many were. It was Day Two of the World's Columbian Exposition, and everybody who was anybody was on the fairgrounds, seeing the event of a lifetime.

There was a silent beat between us. A long one.

"Well," I said. "You keep talking with *that* kind of conviction, I might actually believe you for a change."

He moved to a chair and sat. Heavily. I moved to the bed — distant enough to give him space, not so far as to imply disinterest. His posture slumped: head low, shoulders rounded. I perched with elbows on my knees, hands clasped.

"The vampire you see inside me," Dracula finally said, "is my maker."

I waited, knowing there was more.

He looked up. On his face, for the very first time, I saw the real man beneath all his showmanship and makeup.

"Maker of Eugene," he went on, "and progeny of Amadeus Macht."

TWENTY-THREE

MAKER'S MAKER

Annabel frowned. *"Macht?* Isn't that the vampire who turned Celeste?"

"He didn't turn her," Maurice said. "I turned her. But Macht claimed to know who nearly killed her before I entered the picture."

"But that's whose blood was in the vial Dracula offered you, wasn't it?" Annabel said. "It was a vial of Macht's blood."

"Yes," Maurice said, "but nothing about that vial made sense to me until the day after Tatiana vanished. For one, how did Dracula know I'd be interested in it? He could wave his hands all day about 'sensing my desire for knowledge,' but in truth it always smelled like bullshit. I couldn't shake the feeling that he knew more than he was letting on, even then. But then on top of that, he insisted Tatiana drink some of Macht's blood in addition to his own blood. Why?"

"You said it was for camouflage."

Maurice's mouth twisted, puzzling. "Yeah, but that never really made much sense, either. I went along with it because I figured there was no harm. If anything, Macht's blood would give Tatiana more knowledge about vampires. She needed all she could get for her little crash course."

"So are you saying Dracula had another reason for giving Macht's blood to Tatiana?"

"He did. He was hoping for two things: insight and protection."

"Or so you assume," Annabel said.

"So I *know*," Maurice corrected. "Macht made a vampire named Ophelia, and Ophelia made Eugene-slash-Dracula. That meant Macht was Dracula's *maker's* maker. Dracula was only one degree removed from Macht himself, and that meant he already had Macht's blood in him."

"What does that have to do with 'insight and protection'?"

Maurice stood. He went for a glass of water, then sipped it by the bar.

"There were things about Macht that Dracula wanted to know — things he could *sense*, but not fully understand. Things, as it turned out, that may have drawn him to Chicago and ultimately drew me to him. But there was a problem. See, blood ties are different for everyone. I'm very good at it. I can see intense detail in the memories of my vampire relatives, and I can see pretty far down into my family tree. As I think I told you, my newest progeny Reginald makes me look like an amateur. I can only imagine how far down the tree *he* can go. But other vampires aren't good at blood ties at all. They can't get the hang of it, or they can't separate the memories of others from their own memories, or they can only see fuzzy shapes but nothing concrete. That's how it was for Dracula. He knew there was something in his granddaddy vampire — Macht — that felt very important, but he couldn't see—"

"Important in what way?" Annabel interrupted.

"Important to Holmes. See, what Dracula told me after I finally got him talking was that Ophelia (Dracula's maker and Macht's progeny) was bad from the start. She was power-hungry and ruthless. It was Ophelia who killed Macht, that day after he spiked Celeste's drink with his blood and left us that note. And it was Ophelia who nearly killed Celeste before I came along and saved her."

Annabel sat up, watching Maurice as he returned to the couch. That, she hadn't seen coming.

"So you'd found the vampire you were after. The one who haunted Celeste's dreams."

Maurice nodded, swallowing his last sip before responding. "Yes. Nice little coincidence, right?"

"Are you saying it *wasn't* actually a coincidence?"

Maurice shook his head. "Not at all. Because the other thing Dracula told me was that Ophelia wasn't strong enough to kill Macht by herself. She was over five hundred years old by then, but Macht was nearly a thousand. He was twice as strong and twice as fast. So, like any good schemer, she found some help."

"What help?"

"A necromancer."

Annabel couldn't find words. That, she hadn't expected either.

"I didn't know the details," Maurice went on. "Dracula just told me what he'd seen in those fuzzy blood memories of his, and it went like this: Ophelia and the necromancer partnered up. The necromancer used his abilities to stun Macht, and then Ophelia went in for the kill. But here's the important part: After it was done, Ophelia killed the necromancer to erase the trail."

"Why didn't he use his abilities on Ophelia the way he had on Macht? Stop her from hurting him?"

"He did. But Ophelia knew the trick to defeating a necromancer. She'd known it all along — well before she partnered with the man she intended to kill once the job was done."

"What's the trick?" Annabel asked.

"That," Maurice said, "was exactly Dracula's problem before we met. He knew what had happened between his maker and *her* maker. He knew about the necromancer, and after asking around knew that what Ophelia did — defying a man who was able to control the dead — was something nobody really knew how to do. But in the way of blood hunches, he just kept asking, kept following his nose. It was curiosity at first: a desire to understand his origins, which anyone adopted as a child will tell you can be compelling. Ophelia wasn't a very good maker. She was homicidal, insane, just wanting to kill and pillage. Remember how I said I saw a domineering man in Dracula's memories, like a father who never spared the rod? Turns out, it wasn't a man at all. It was *Ophelia* who made his life a living Hell before he escaped under a tarp, using the cover of daylight. I'd just assumed she was a father figure, not a Mommie Dearest. Is that sexist?"

"Quite," said Annabel, but she said it with a smile. Then she shifted to the loose end he'd dangled earlier. "You still haven't told me what any of that has to do with Dracula insisting Tatiana drink Macht's blood. You said it was for ..."

Maurice nodded. "Insight and protection. Right. I told you Dracula was bad at blood ties, but wanted to know more. Specifically, after he encountered Holmes and realized he was a necromancer, he wanted to know how Ophelia had managed to disobey and kill one so that Dracula, in turn, could disobey and kill Holmes. See, he had that intent all along — that *noble* intent to rid the world of a monster. He wasn't a bad guy. *Isn't* a bad guy, because as far as I know, he's still alive. He's just a fool, scarred and frightened by his vampire childhood with Ophelia. Sometimes a coward. He knew the knowledge was in Macht's blood, though, even though Macht was dead by the time Ophelia killed the necromancer. Blood ties are recursive. Once Ophelia knew, some part of Macht knew ... and his blood *still* knew, even in 1893. But the problem was, Dracula couldn't drink the vial of blood and learn any of what he needed from Macht's blood. How could he? He was Macht's grandchild. He *already* had Macht in him, and the memories he needed weren't going to get any clearer with a tiny bit more blood. To learn what he wanted to learn, Dracula needed to give the blood to another vampire. One who was better at reading blood than he was."

"You," Annabel said.

"Only as a last resort," Maurice answered. "He didn't want to give me the vial until he absolutely had to. He knew I'd be angry. He carried a lot of guilt — some of it justified, some not. It wasn't his fault that his maker nearly killed my wife, but he *had* hidden that information from me. So he gave the blood to Tatiana, then gave her hints when I wasn't around. He suggested she look deep into Macht's blood, hoping she'd see the necromancer and how Ophelia had killed him. If she could see in the blood what Dracula couldn't, that'd give us an edge against Holmes."

Annabel nodded, understanding. *Insight* (about his past) and *protection* (from the necromancer).

"How did Dracula *get* the vial of blood?" she asked. "If Macht was already dead by the time Dracula ran away from Ophelia—"

"Ophelia had a collection. Trophies, in a way. I told you she was crazy. I think Dracula stole that vial from her stash on a whim, sure only that he wanted to 'know more' in some dark corner of his mind. But I also think he tucked it away somewhere once he'd escaped, maybe forgetting until I showed up and he started putting pieces together. The vampire world is a small one. Dracula was born in America, but Ophelia came over from Europe just after Columbus."

Annabel let it settle. Then she said, "There's just one thing I don't understand. You said that Dracula gave Tatiana some of Macht's blood because he thought it could give her an advantage — and, if he was lucky, help him learn more about his roots than he could figure out on his own."

"Right."

"But you also said that Dracula asked you to drink *his* blood instead of Tatiana's."

"Because he wanted to get caught, deep down. Or maybe he knew, deep down, that I'd need to know it all to help us out of the situation he was getting us into. Vampires have subconscious minds just like humans do. You, as a therapist, must understand the way we sometimes do things we don't think we want to do."

"I do understand," Annabel said. "But if you had Dracula's blood in you the day Tatiana went missing ..."

"Yeah ..."

"... and if Tatiana had *Macht's* blood in *her* ..."

"Go on."

"Then shouldn't you have had access to Macht's memories after all, even though you didn't drink Macht's blood directly?"

Maurice smiled: a puzzle well-solved.

"The exact thing you've explained," he said, "occurred to me just before dusk."

TWENTY-FOUR
TRANSITIVE BLOOD

I WAS NEVER good at math. I was good enough, though, to know that if A equals B and B equals C, then by virtue of some property I don't recall or care about, A must equal C as well.

That's the way it can be with blood, for talented readers like myself. In the case of May 1893, it very much was. It dawned on me after Dracula told his tale, after the awkward and empty silence that followed. Both of us were drained to the point of exhaustion. We'd shared a wino on the way home, but his blood hadn't been robust and both of us soon felt the wino's loginess as our own. Dracula had slept a little while I invaded his dreams, and I hadn't slept at all. After the confessions began, our energy was sapped further — Dracula's by the soul-searching required for coming clean, mine from arguments and trying to comprehend. By seven o'clock that afternoon we were a pair of undead dishrags. A weakling could have staked us both with chopsticks.

"Let's go over it again," I said.

"Let's not," Dracula replied. "We've been over it and over it and over it."

I shrugged. At sunrise, I would have argued with him. I would have pushed him around. But now that Dracula had given me everything, we were equals. I couldn't shove anymore without being shoved back. I couldn't insult his stupid outfits anymore without expecting a jab at my mop-head in return.

"It's almost sunset," he said. "We can go out and look again then."

My spirit was willing, but my flesh and will had gone weak. I understood intellectually that Tatiana's life hung in the balance. I knew, on a rational level, that she was likely still alive and that if we found her, we could save her. It'd still take some doing, but at this point I was willing to do whatever it took, even if it ended up jailing us and letting Holmes escape. All that mattered was finding Tatiana.

But I was just so tired.

"Fine," I said.

It was hard to summon optimism. Everything looked so bleak. Holmes hadn't returned to the hotel, but Wyatt, using the delicate lock-pick of a sledgehammer, had broken his way into Holmes's other abode and come over to tell us that it, too, was empty.

"They must still be at the fair," said Dracula.

"Why?"

"Because it's the only place left."

Which was so logically flawed as to be laughable. He acted as if there were only three locations in the world: Holmes's property plus the fair. In truth, there were billions of others. Trains took people to them all the time.

Dracula sat up from his slouch. "I'm serious. They had a long list of exhibits they wanted to see. It was open all night for opening day only. Why's it so crazy to think they might have just stuck around?"

"Even if that's true," I said, "how are we supposed to find them? There are dozens of large buildings. Acres and acres of lands, paths, and canals. Thousands of exhibits. Humans in this city all dress the same. Even Tatiana was in long sleeves, covering her tattoos. If he's actively hiding, Lord knows how many little nooks and crannies there are. There's no way to search it all. Not in time."

"So you just want to give up?"

I sat up now, too. If he was going to get righteous, I guess I needed to engage.

"You can't even help me narrow it down. You don't know which exhibits they wanted to visit. Think hard. You can't be more specific?"

He thought. "No."

"Don't just try to remember what you saw last night. Look into your blood memories *now*. You should be able to read something that recent like a book."

"*You* can," Dracula said. "You know I'm not as good at that stuff as you."

I did. It was one of a hundred things we'd spent the sleepless day beating to death.

I blinked. Something occurring to me.

"What do you know about a book?" I asked, recalling something I'd seen in his blood many hours before.

"A book?"

"When you opened your mind yesterday, I saw a book inside your memories. A huge, old, yellowed volume, like something off the Gutenberg press."

Dracula shrugged.

"What significant books were in your life?"

"I really enjoyed *Pride and Prejudice*."

"Not that kind of book."

He shook his head.

I stood. Now that I'd cracked the topic, it felt like a vein of ore I'd do well to mine deeper. "It felt older than you," I said. "Maybe it was one of Tatiana's memories. Everything was kind of mashed together, as if your head was a trash heap."

"Tatiana is younger than me."

I squinted, resisting a block. Then I had it. That math property — *transitive*, I think. *If A is equal to B and B is equal to C, A must be equal to C.* Only for me, in the moment, it went like this: *If I'm connected to Dracula and Dracula is connected to Tatiana and Tatiana is, by virtue of drinking that vial, connected to Amadeus Macht, then I must be connected to Macht.*

The memory of the book might be Macht's. Or — and this felt right, if four layers distant — *Ophelia's.*

Oh, and what about the closer nearby memory I hadn't fully explored? In the same blink as the book memory, I'd seen two fingers on a map, two fingers scanning a list of exhibits. That had to be Tatiana's mind, just before it turned to blackness. And even though Dracula's ability wouldn't let him see detail in that list of exhibits, there was no reason my better ability couldn't.

"I just realized," I told Dracula, "you don't need to remember. I can."

"You can?"

I nodded. "And I can remember beyond her. You gave her Macht's blood. Through her, I can see that, too."

Now Dracula really sat up. "You can see *Macht?*"

Looking inward, I blinked around the room like a blind man. "I think I can even see Ophelia."

I tried to focus, feeling my touch slip each time I endeavored to see more. Seeing into Dracula was easy. Seeing into Tatiana through Dracula was harder. Seeing into Macht was harder still and seeing into Ophelia — hundreds of years ago, filtered through psychosis and Macht's death — was nearly impossible. It was like trying to study a painting over which the artist had painted another.

"Are you serious?"

I nodded. "I'm pretty sure ..." I stopped, re-gripped, then began again more confidently. "I'm pretty sure the memory of the book was hers. It's even harder to see than normal because I'm seeing it through Macht, and Ophelia did her best to hide that particular memory from Macht before she killed him. But it's there."

"*And?*"

"It has something to do with the necromancer."

"Really? What book is it? What does it say?"

I tried a bit longer, then shook my head. "I don't know. I could describe it, but that doesn't help us."

But a funny sensation still prickled beneath my skin, waiting to be acknowledged. There were two Edison wires inside my head, sparking as they tried to connect. I was sure there was more to this feeling washing through me — *much more* — but I couldn't find all the pieces.

Following my gut, I zeroed in on Tatiana's vision. I looked at the map she'd seen with her own eyes, watching her own fingers, reading the list of fair exhibits. But what did that have to do with anything?

The book.

The fair.

The necromancer.

Dammit, somehow it all connected.

No longer seeing Dracula as I focused on the memory, I said, "You told me Holmes was interested in visiting exhibits about folklore. Ones having to do with mythology and ... and *artifacts?*"

Dracula replied, now just a voice-over for the vision playing in my head. "Something like that."

"You studied Holmes before I arrived. You said you couldn't get close enough to find anything about Emeline. That was meant to be my job. But if you studied him, you must know something of the man. Enough to know he's a doctor. Enough to know he's a dichrome."

"I found out he was a dichrome when I tried to glamour him myself."

"Enough to know he's a necromancer."

The book.

Mythology and folklore.

The necromancer.

The book.

The BOOK.

I was at the tip of something. I stopped moving, as if the elusive idea might see my movements and run away.

"During your studies," I said, "did you ever hear of Holmes having any interest in folklore? Any at all?"

"No. But that doesn't mean—"

I held up a finger. I was focused on Tatiana's finger as she'd scanned the exhibit list. No, no ... I turned my attention to Holmes's finger. *His* was the finger that mattered. I was manipulating bits of the image, letting my mind fall into the intuitive interspace behind all blood ties. Each movement sharpened the text. Each movement got me closer to seeing which exhibits Holmes had wanted so badly to see. Because Dracula was right, even if his declaration didn't help: It *wasn't* logical for Holmes to leave Chicago, or to go to places unknown within it. Until Tatiana became obviously vampire, Holmes would have no idea we were plotting against him. He should still believe she'd be boarding a train out of town tomorrow — and that meant if he wanted to have sex with or kill her, it'd need to happen tonight. Such an innocent tryst (innocent for Holmes, at least) would portend no danger. He'd have no reason to leave town, no reason to hide. No reason to kill Tatiana anywhere but at the castle, where he'd be comfortable and in control. If he was anywhere right now, he'd be at the fair. But why? Tatiana had been flirting when the lights went out, trying to lure him back so he could spring his trap on her — after which, of course, we could spring one right back on him. Why would Holmes resist? What at the fair, I had to wonder, could interest Holmes enough to supercede the thrill of sex and murder?

With my mind's eye, I watched Holmes's finger stop on an exhibit entitled: *Artifacts of Legend: The Primitive World's Battle with Ghosts and Spirits.*

And I thought, *Artifacts.*

And I thought, *Ghosts and Spirits.*

And I thought, *The book.*

And I understood.

I gave it a moment, letting the pieces of the four-layer puzzle settle before daring to move my mind elsewhere. But I didn't need to worry; once I had those two important elements (the book and the notion of spirits) the rest slotted into place with the rigidity of a girder.

I opened my inner eyes, returning them to my outer eyes. Dracula was in front of me, waiting on bated breath.

"Ophelia disarmed the necromancer with an incantation from an ancient text," I said.

"The book you saw in her memory?"

I nodded. "Holmes knows. Maybe from his study of necromancy or maybe some other way, but he *knows.*"

"He knows about Ophelia?"

I shook my head. "He knows there's a copy of that book

on display at the Columbian Exhibition. He knows it's the only copy left. It's the only thing that could prevent him from controlling vampires for the rest of his piddly human life." I looked at Dracula, feeling the weight of what I was about to say as if it were just now occurring to me.

"And when the fair closes tonight," I said, "he's going to destroy it."

History proved H. H. Holmes to be a firebug. When he had evidence he needed to hide or something he needed to destroy, he simply burned it down. He started a lab fire to disfigure Pitezel's body after murdering him later on, and may have set the fire that consumed much of his own hotel. I knew none of that the second night of the fair, but now I think that was his plan: to set fire to not just the Artifacts exhibit after the fair was closed and security dwindled to a minimum, but to the whole damned building. He'd start with that big book I'd seen in my mind — that enormous, yellow-paged, druid-age volume that told the curious how to disarm his kind. It'd be easy. God knows the expo's rushed construction made it a burner just waiting to happen.

That made me wonder if perhaps Holmes knew our plan after all.

The moment the sun dipped below the horizon, Dracula and I rushed to the gate, taking the building-hopping route I'd taken the night before. He left his cape and medal and leapt with strength I didn't know he had. We made it to the gate, leapt it, then hustled with all the rapidity we could muster for the Manufactures and Liberal Arts Building where a fair guide told us the artifacts exhibit was kept.

We still didn't have all the answers. We didn't know why Holmes had taken Tatiana on his burning errand, and we didn't know why he didn't wait until the next day, when he'd have been done with her. We didn't know why, of all times, he'd chosen *now*. I had a guess, but it was only that: Holmes had a fastidious, obsessive personality, so if he knew a book existed that could ruin his influence, he'd probably been chasing it down for years. Once he'd heard it would be coming to Chicago for the fair, he must have decided to rid the world of it at the first opportunity — which, of course, would be the first closing night.

But something in my gut bothered me about that explanation. We'd been operating as if Holmes was a simple human murderer chasing simple human prey, but even his study of necromancy said different. Nobody is born a necromancer; it's something that must be studied — and it's *hard* to study, with few experts still around. A man doesn't go to that kind of effort if he's ignorant. He doesn't learn to charm the dead if he doesn't believe the dead walk the Earth. He *certainly* doesn't track down an ancient book with the ability to rob him of his ability if he doesn't believe he has an ability, or that the book could stop him. So I had to ask: Had we figured Holmes all wrong?

If we had, the implications were frightening.

It meant he knew vampires existed, even though we'd been assuming him ignorant.

It meant he knew I was one of them.

It could easily mean that he knew we were after him. His rush to the fair's Artifacts exhibit backed the idea up: If Maurice Toussant had a plan, might Maurice not be searching for ways to defeat him — ways like a book with the power to disarm necromancers?

But worst of all — if Holmes was familiar with vampires and saw a vampire plot against him — it might mean that he knew Tatiana was one. We might not have fooled him at all. He might know she wasn't just a silly broken girl he could abuse and exploit. He might, after the book was gone and the next morning dawned with Tatiana entirely vampire, be planning to keep her at the fair. To keep her on the promenade, in the bright light of day.

Or, he might have finished her already. In-between as Tatiana was, sunlight wouldn't kill her. Gas wouldn't, a knife wouldn't, a bullet wouldn't. But cutting off her head? A stake through the heart? Those things killed both vampires *and* humans.

We still didn't know why Tatiana had blacked out. Her death, improbable as it was, remained the best explanation. So had he done it right there in front of everyone? Staked her through the back, then dragged her off claiming she was ill?

The thought made me shiver.

"How are we going to do this, Maurice?" Dracula asked as we neared the target building. It was five minutes to closing, so we entered through the front door. A guard told us the exhibits were about to close, but I told him we'd lost my friend's pocketwatch and would be back before the lock turned. Instead, we vanished into the exhibits. The guard, distracted by the fair's crowd, forgot all about us.

"I don't know," I said. "I'm clinging to one thing that gives me hope. The only thing we know for sure."

"Which is?"

"Necromancer or not, he's still human."

It was little comfort. I still had no idea how we were

going to move against even an ordinary, mortal human if we were already conditioned against it. He could be shot by a robber, but couldn't be touched by us. We couldn't call police, or call for help, or anything of the sort. The best idea on the table was to hint Wyatt into lighting the building on fire before Holmes could, barring the doors with all of us inside. Wyatt, too, was a bit of a firebug.

There were downsides to that plan: our deaths, Tatiana's death, the distinct possibility that the fire would spread across the fairgrounds. But so far it was all we had.

We hid until the lights went out. We heard the door lock. Then we skulked like catburglars, crouched and rushing on tiptoes from exhibit to exhibit.

In the dim, the collection of ancient artifacts spooked me to the core. Dracula, too.

"Look, Maurice. Shrunken heads."

I looked. There were still tribes that did such things. Tribes that mounted heads on sticks and ate flesh, too.

I didn't reply. He kept pointing things out. I didn't reply to any of those, either.

I kept moving, eyes peeled for the book. I had no idea where it would be, but I knew that Holmes, if he had half a brain, would use it as tinder. You didn't start a fire to destroy something but leave the destruction to chance. No — you started with the thing that needed to go. The target was where you touched the flame. If I wanted to find Holmes, that's where I needed to begin: where the fire began.

Dracula was lagging. I waved at him, but he didn't see me. I hissed low, but he didn't hear me. So I rushed to his side, seeing him stare at a display that turned my insides to ice.

There were models and sketches of a creature more hideous than all the ghosts and specters we'd passed so far.

It was like an upright elk, massive, its body in decay, its teeth — canines like ours, not typically found on elk — visible through gums like macerated meat. Front and center, laid beneath the drawings, was an amulet. It wasn't unlike the medal Dracula usually wore.

"Wendigo," he said. "Eater of flesh."

"We need to go," I said. "I think I hear someone ahead."

"'Ancients believed that this amulet,'" he read off a placard inside the case, "'allowed a wendigo to possess its victims and take them over.'"

"Dracula," I said, taking his shoulder. He jumped as if he hadn't seen me.

He turned. "Eugene," he said.

"*Eugene.* We can't be seen. Not until we ..." Well, I wasn't sure *what* exactly we were going to do when the moment came to be seen. I left the sentence unfinished.

"Maurice?"

"Yes."

His eyes ticked to the roomful of creepy displays. The only light came from a skylight far above, showing the glow from string lights on the walkways below. He stopped at the wendigo display, then met my eyes and spoke again. I saw new depth there. I saw terror.

"I'm scared."

"I know." A footstep, echoing just one or two rooms away. "But you have to swallow it."

I took his arm and led him. We rushed on soft feet until we were against a wall with an arched doorway into the next room.

I peeked.

Then, not trusting myself to speak aloud and not trusting Eugene's facility with blood ties, I dropped into pantomime.

I pointed at my eyes and then around the corner: *I see something*. I held up two fingers: *Two people*. Then I nodded: *The ones we're looking for: Holmes and Tatiana*.

He relaxed at that. She was still in peril, and we still had no way to defeat Holmes even if he was too glamoured to hurt us. But at least the first question was answered: He hadn't killed her.

Then I saw the book. It was in a display opposite. My vampire eyes could easily read the headline written on the wall behind it: *A Handbook for Manipulation of the Dead*.

I made a "book" pantomime and pointed. Eugene nodded.

Then a voice split the darkness.

"Mr. Toussant. It is so grand to see you again."

I gave Eugene a nod to stay put, then walked out. Holmes was beneath the skylight, Tatiana in hand.

"Fancy meeting you here," he said once he saw me.

"Really? *That's* the line you're going with?" said Tatiana. His knuckles were white on her flesh. It had to hurt, the way he'd restrained her. How long had he held her? It'd been more than a day since she'd gone missing.

"Are you okay?" I shouted to Tatiana.

"Peachy."

"She's fine," said Holmes, "and still very much human."

"So you know," I said.

Holmes nodded. "I know."

I tried to make myself run at him. My feet were rooted. The necromancer's spell was in me like a tapeworm.

"Can't quite do it, can you?" Holmes asked, watching me stall. He had that giant walrus mustache and was rudely wearing his familiar bowler hat. When his head ticked away, I looked at the book. All my ideas concerning it were pointless. Even if I could get to the thing, his curse wouldn't let me read from it.

"Let her go," I said.

"Why?"

It was a good question.

"It's fine, Maurice," said Tatiana. "I got this."

Of course, she didn't. At all. She didn't yet have vampire strength. If he could hold onto her now, he'd hold her for the duration.

"You should go," Holmes said. "Leave me with her."

"You don't even need her. Let her go, and we'll let you do what you came here to do."

"Perhaps you misunderstand. What I came here to do requires this fine young woman."

"Go back to your hotel," I said. "I won't try and stop you."

Holmes laughed. His eyes took in the surroundings. We were in a rotunda, the walls a giant circle. The dome yawned above us, even our quiet voices making echoes.

"You read about standoffs in fiction," said Holmes. "Grand pronunciations. Taunts. I never thought I'd see one play out. Is this the part where I need to explain that you have no leverage, and I hold all the cards?"

"No," said Tatiana, "this is the part where I kick you in the balls."

Holmes turned his head — possibly to ask a well-mannered *"What?"* — but Tatiana's foot was already in motion. Once the foot was launched, I realized she'd been tensing it from the moment I'd entered the room. Holmes, if he'd had the confidence to call my name, had probably been blabbing about how dumb I'd be to come and face him. Tatiana must have made a counter-plan, and stood prepared.

Her kick was a piece of testicular-bashing art. She was wearing pointed dress boots and an elaborate outfit Holmes must have dressed her in, and to my eye the combination made for a flourish like a magician's trick. The boot rose on bent knee; the leg straightened; her starched petticoats rustled as if in applause. Her toe contacted Holmes's left ball, which my eyes had no problem outlining through his trousers. The upper — where the laces were — deftly mashed the other. Seeing it all in slow motion, I tuned into the sounds that came next: a sharp intake of air as Holmes took his nut-based trauma, the slippery, meat-mallet sound of his balls mashing under pressure, a satisfying "oof" and then no voice at all as Holmes buckled and lost his wind. He hit the deck on his ass.

As the beauty unfolded, I watched a slo-mo smile bloom on Tatiana's face. For all his planning and ghost-charming abilities, he'd forgotten that one boot in the jimmies could trump it all.

Tatiana shook free as Holmes fell, though it was a narrow thing; he'd clung tight enough to almost drag her with him. Then she was off and running, human speed, while Holmes tried to recover. I leapt to get between them, but my feet fought to betray me. Holmes saw. He laughed, even while cupping his scrotum. It came out like a cough.

My only hope was that she could outrun him and find an exit, because it seemed this charmed vampire wasn't going to be any help.

Holmes got to knees, then feet. Still wincing, he shambled after her. I could shuffle a little under Holmes's spell, but mostly I only watched.

I watched Tatiana dart into a room off the alcove, wincing, knowing it was a single chamber: a dead end.

She realized right away, but by the time she was coming

back out to try for another door, Holmes had found his feet. He parked himself ten feet from her, and together they entered the shuffling standoff that happens when one person means for another not to pass.

"I like a girl with some fight in her," Holmes said, grinning.

He lunged. Tatiana, seemingly a one-trick pony, tried again to whack his danglers. She caught him sidelong: no real damage. It let her get past him and nothing more. Holmes countered; they again hit a standoff, this time with a table display between them. I stood like a fool statue, observing it all.

"Go on," he said. "Keep running. I have all the time in the world."

I heard a rustling from behind us. Holmes, with slower human reflexes, heard it a second later, and by then the rustle had turned into a whoosh. Movement caught my eye and at first I thought a tiny trolley car was moving across the floor as part of the expo's magic. If I saw the same thing today, I'd think it was a miniature Zamboni.

But it wasn't a mini trolley or a mini Zamboni. It was the big old book, sliding across the floor on its covers and spine — open wide, as if the ceiling meant to read it.

It slid under the table and stopped against Tatiana's shoe. She looked down, then past me. I turned my head to see that it was Dracula — Eugene — who'd taken the book from its case and slid it to her.

"Halfway down the left page," was all Eugene said.

Tatiana stooped. Holmes's eyes widened.

"What are you doing?" he said, a new emotion in his voice. Confusion? Or fear?

She stood with it, keeping it open. The table was between them. Holmes flinched left and Tatiana flinched left. He flinched right and she flinched right. Every time he went for her, she darted away.

Keeping one eye on Holmes, she started to read aloud what neither Eugene nor I could have. We were vampires and Holmes was human. Tatiana, on the other hand, was something else — and for now at least, free to act against her master.

She read. It didn't take long. It was one sentence, maybe two. I didn't understand the language, and Tatiana clearly didn't speak it. When she was done, Holmes stood dumbfounded. Still he leapt. He made it only halfway across the table, so Tatiana did the most logical thing: she closed the big book and hit him so hard over the head with it, I heard it rack his jaw into the marble below.

I looked at Eugene. At Tatiana. Then I lunged toward her to hustle her to safety, but I was so surprised that she beat me to it. Holmes was unconscious, maybe even dead. As Tatiana came around and rushed to me before I could rush to her, I turned my attention to her. Holmes wasn't going anywhere fast.

I embraced her. Eugene joined us, and suddenly we were all in a massive hug.

I broke it, then turned to Holmes.

"She killed him," Eugene said.

To that I replied, "She didn't kill him enough."

I tensed to finish the job now that the necromancy was lifted, but I heard a loud bang first. It was coming from the entrance. After that came many footsteps, rushed and heavy-footed. I knew: It was police. Then there were more footsteps, faster than the rest, and the shout of a familiar voice.

It screamed, *"Right this fucking way, fuckheads!"*

"It's Wyatt," said Tatiana.

"How?"

"He knows everything about what we're doing here. All the freaks do."

I eyed the door. The opposite door. Tatiana saw it and nodded. "Yes," she said.

"Yes what?"

"Yes, we need to go."

"Why?"

"Because the police wouldn't listen to the freaks. You know that."

I gave the cacophony coming toward us another half-beat.

"He's not leading them, Maurice," Tatiana said, now grabbing my sleeve and tugging. "They're chasing him."

I understood. Wyatt, seemingly in collusion with Tatiana, had taken a gamble. The cops wouldn't go after Holmes on the say-so of a bunch of sideshow freaks, but they were willing to *arrest* freaks if they did something like, say, pulling down the skirts of six or seven fairgoers and shouting about it. The cops would catch Wyatt for sure, but if he got lucky, they'd catch Holmes, too. His unconscious ass would be found trespassing, and I was willing to bet his pockets were full of evidence. Half the creditors in town would come to his hearing so long as he had one, just to tell how this smooth man bilked them.

You can't outrun your deeds forever. That was something Dr. Holmes was about to learn, just as Wyatt was about to learn you couldn't outrun cops on legs half the length of theirs.

"*Now*, you two," Tatiana said, "or Wyatt's done this for nothing."

We slipped out, breathing heavy.

I stayed at the door long enough to peek through the gap and watch them put Holmes's slumped form in handcuffs.

"He's alive," I said. "Unfortunately."

"It's all right," said Tatiana. "I slipped something into his pocket."

"What?"

"One of Mamie's letters. One of the most tearful. She wrote me that she knew Julia was dead, and that the man who ran the hotel she'd stayed at — that horrible Dr. Holmes — topped her list of suspects."

"Then it may be time for an anonymous tip about searching the castle. After seeing that note, maybe they'll actually listen," Eugene said. "Come on. There's a phone we can use two blocks away."

We walked there. Leisurely. Human speeds. I hated that Wyatt's intrusion had kept me from killing Holmes, but I was happy to know he'd get his justice.

When we reached the phone, I picked up the candle-stick and put the speaker to my ear. I had all sorts of things to tell the police about Holmes and what I'd found in his basement, and planned to spill every bit now that the necromancer's spell had been broken.

But once the desk sergeant was on the line, I found myself unable to speak. No matter how hard I tried to rat Holmes out, my lips wouldn't move.

TWENTY-SIX

POINTLESS

"It didn't work?" Annabel asked.

Maurice shook his head. "No. Whatever kept me from going after Holmes, it stayed firmly in place. I tried to visit him while they held him for a day, but I couldn't get close. I tried to talk to authorities several times, but I couldn't speak. Same for Eugene."

"Why?"

"I don't know. Maybe the thing with the book was a farce. But since I'd seen Ophelia use it on her necromancer, I'm pretty sure it wasn't. My best guess is that Tatiana got the pronunciations wrong. It was in some weird dead language. Afterward, I compared my memory of Tatiana saying the words to Ophelia, and they weren't exactly the same. It must have needed to be *exactly* the same. I tried to coach her to say it right, but by then my body had mostly metabolized Eugene's blood. I couldn't reach the Ophelia memory after that."

"You said the police held Holmes for a day?"

Maurice nodded. There was a sadness in that nod — not the triumph the conclusion of this story deserved. Annabel had already read up on this part, and she'd known in advance of Maurice's story that Holmes hadn't been convicted in '93. She wasn't surprised, but somehow she'd hoped reality might actually be different.

"They cited him for trespassing, but it was just a ticketable offense. They found Mamie's letter in his pocket, and the freaks did what I'd tried to do: pile up the evidence to compel the police to search the castle. But Holmes was smooth and had a good lawyer and in the end our hunch had been right: Nobody listened to freaks. Certainly not against a charmer like Holmes."

"What about his creditors? You said he owed money to everyone. How did that not catch up with him?"

"It did, but only years later. They eventually jailed him for fraud, and while he was in prison, a detective named Frank Geyer found evidence he'd murdered the Pitezel family." Maurice took a breath. "All of them."

Annabel sat back. It shouldn't have been crushing to hear something she'd already known about, but somehow it was. The wind left her sails. She'd let herself rise on the momentum of Maurice's story, sure somehow that he and the others would prevail. But no. Holmes hadn't just lived; he'd remained a free man. He'd spent the rest of the Chicaco fair right where he'd been, surely murdering others while the world went right on by.

"I should have killed him, that day in the Manufactures and Liberal Arts Building."

"You couldn't, if you were still under his spell."

"I should have taken the book. Coached Tatiana to say the incantation correctly, right there on the spot."

"You didn't know, Maurice," Annabel said.

"You asked if I'd ever killed innocents," he said. "The answer is yes. Yes I have, by failing to stop him."

"It's not the same. Holmes killed his victims, not you. We all have to do the best with what we have — even vampires. Living forever doesn't make your judgment perfect. Far from it."

His head bobbed. He'd clearly thought a lot about this. It had, she realized, plagued him.

She decided to change the subject. What was, *was*. It couldn't be changed. But that didn't mean there weren't some victories along the way.

"What happened to Dracula and Tatiana?" she asked.

Too late, she realized she didn't already know, and that they might have met tragic ends. Fortunately, her redirect hit the mark. Maurice's face brightened.

"They're both fine, as far as I know. Dracula dropped the act and became plain old Eugene Dupree. I don't keep in touch with either of them anymore, but I hear they keep in touch with each other, as maker and progeny."

"Father and daughter?"

"Well," said Maurice, "I wouldn't go that far."

But, Annabel thought, she herself might. Maurice hadn't talked much about Tatiana's past, but she felt safe betting that it wasn't great. Dracula — Eugene, in the end — sounded like an abused child of the vampire variety. If they'd bonded at all — found family at all — it was a plus in Annabel's book.

"And," Maurice volunteered, "the whole thing gave Eugene a bit of a breakthrough. I told you how he slid the book to Tatiana? He'd given her exactly the right page, and the book was enormous. Isn't that interesting?"

"That *is* interesting. How did he know where inside the book to find the spell?"

"He told me later that he saw Ophelia turn to that page in a very old memory, and read that passage."

Annabel nodded with a small smile. Somehow, Dracula had gotten better at blood ties when it mattered — even if in the end, none of it had mattered much.

"Did Eugene honor your deal? Did he give you the vial?"

"There was no need. By the word of our deal, I'd uncovered no concrete proof at all — not about Julia, not about Emeline, not even about Minnie and Nannie, who'd been snatched from right beneath our noses. That evidence came later. I'll leave it to you and the internet to look it up, if you'd like." He sighed. "Besides, I'd seen all I needed to see through Eugene and Tatiana's blood, and told Celeste later what I knew. She still has her problems, but at least now we know what's in that black trunk inside her mind. The spook in her dreams is Ophelia, who nearly killed her as a human."

"What *about* Ophelia? Is she still around?"

Maurice's eyes darkened. "Yes. She's still around."

There was a long silence — the kind that usually meant Maurice was at his limit. Annabel felt the hypnosis of storytelling depart and her usual hypnosis replace it. Her mind formed its schism. She began to store what Maurice had told her inside her mind, locked behind patient confidentiality — but in the same moment, her mind opened, knowing she'd tell her horrible husband everything whether she wanted to or not. After that, he'd give his usual marching orders. And so it would go, unseen and unspoken.

Annabel uncrossed her legs and set her notepad aside. Maurice sat up, then looked at her without speaking.

"You seem bothered," he said.

"Hearing about serial killers will do that."

"I'm sorry."

"Don't be. I just ..."

"What?"

"Somehow, even knowing the history, I hoped you might have caught him." She took a breath, then added something that wasn't strictly professional. "... and killed him."

She shouldn't have said that. Maurice shook his head, defeat returning.

"If only. Holmes got his in the end, but not for three more years. You know the people he murdered even after we entered his life ... then left it without having done a damn thing."

"You can't blame yourself," Annabel said.

"I guess I don't. But it's hard. I was in America for a few more months, trying to stop him. But the spell held, and eventually I gave up and went home to my wife." He shook his head, frustrated all over again. "I don't understand. It should have worked. I've researched a lot since — trying to fix the past, I guess. I can no longer access the memory of Ophelia disabling her necromancer, but I just ... I just *know* that what Tatiana did was close enough! It should have disarmed him. It should have broken his control over me, and let me get close enough to kill him!"

"Maybe it had something to do with the blackout. The way Tatiana's mind just ... vanished."

He was still shaking his head. Annabel's posit made him shake it harder. "I never got an answer to that, either."

"Well," Annabel said, standing as well, "I guess not all monsters have to walk around on goat legs."

He was already halfway to the door, so bothered by this digging-up of the failed past that he'd forgotten even to say goodbye.

"Goat legs?" he said now.

"You know. Like a demon. Legs of a goat? Half human, half animal?"

"Half human," he said, touching his lips. "Half animal."

She tried on a somber smile. "As we all are, I suppose."

He moved toward the door again.

"Maurice?"

He looked back.

"Remember: Just because you have such depth of memory, that doesn't mean you should spend time trying to exhume a past you can't change. Sometimes, our worst days are meant to stay buried."

"'*Stay buried,*'" he said, trying to match her halfway smile. "I'll try to remember that."

Then like a whisper, the vampire was gone.

TWENTY-SEVEN
STAY BURIED

Six miles outside of Philadelphia, in the small town of Landsdowne, Pennsylvania, Maurice pulled his car to the side of the road beside a sign marking the entrance to Holy Cross Cemetery. The night was moonless. In the distance, the lights of the big city lit up the sky, but out here, silence reigned.

He popped the trunk. Inside were two shovels and two pickaxes. The man at the hardware store had joked, asking if he was going mining. The ground here wasn't rocky enough for pickaxes. The soil was lush, made for things that grow.

Except, Maurice thought, for things that refuse to die.

In prior weeks, his appointments with Dr. Rice had left Maurice anywhere from euphoric to melancholy. Either way, the mood passed with the return of the next night sky. This time, the mood had stayed with him — and it was a bitter, vitriolic mood. It had its own vices, its own personality. It gnawed at his dreams, enough that Celeste had to keep waking him for fear of nightmares. It hung behind him wherever he went, even when he fed. It was a constant devil on his shoulder. A nagging loose end. Something not-quite-right, personified.

He remembered Annabel's advice.

You shouldn't spend time trying to exhume a past you can't change. Sometimes, our worst days are meant to stay buried.

Stay buried.

He'd read something online, when he'd been refreshing his memory. Some furor in 2017 had piqued interest in the curious matter of H. H. Holmes, and it'd culminated in just what Annabel had said: an exhumation. They'd dug him up, some amateur sleuth having decided they'd buried the wrong man. Maurice, interest piqued in return, had gone through his Rolodex after that, searching until he found a vampire who knew someone who knew someone who knew someone who'd seen Holmes hanged. The man had been preternaturally calm right through the moment the trapdoor beneath him had sprung: no fear, certainly no sign of remorse. He had, interestingly, looked different in the memory Maurice had borrowed from his vampire friend: gaunt, narrower in face, somehow less round and more ominous than Maurice remembered. With that, he'd recalled something else he'd read about Holmes: that while awaiting execution, he believed he'd come to resemble the devil.

But it wasn't goat legs that Maurice imagined on this satanic Holmes. It was deer legs. *Elk* legs. Antlers, instead of the nubs of tiny goat horns. A rotting body, upright and enormous. A fearful thing, Satan's equal ... but not Satan, that was sure.

With the memory spurned by a drop of donated blood, Maurice had watched Holmes die on May 7 of 1896 at Moyamensing Prison — three years almost to the day from that night at the fair. In 1896, however, Holmes's neck hadn't broken from the first jolt of hanging. He'd dangled from the rope for nearly fifteen minutes, slowly suffocating. Then his legs had kicked a final time and it'd been over.

Maurice carried his burdens: two shovels, in case one broke. It'd taken courage enough to do this once, and he didn't want to need to run out for a shovel and do it again. Two picks, in case one of *those* broke, too. The New England soil was soft and forgiving, but Herman Webster Mudgett — known to the world forever as Dr. H. H. Holmes — had known that, too. Just as he'd stripped bodies to skeletons, so too had he feared others might to do the same to him. So he'd left instructions that he be buried in concrete. Inches of it. Then, atop the slab, he'd left instructions for those who came afterward to pour even more concrete, and do it again.

He kept thinking of what Annabel had said, and about the hauntings people associated with the Holmes case had suffered after he'd died. There'd been random, unexplained deaths. The burning of the castle, as if from nothing. And the questions Maurice had never had answered, and now wondered anew over a hundred years later.

Tatiana had read the passage close enough to correct. Maurice was sure of it. The spell she'd read should have disarmed a necromancer. And what about the blackout — the way Tatiana's blood had vanished from Eugene's mind, then stayed vanished?

Maurice had begun to wonder if Holmes was a necromancer after all. Although if he hadn't, why hadn't Maurice and other vampires been able to act against him?

He thought of the exhumation from 2017. There'd been no DNA forensics to compare back then. They'd identified the man by his teeth.

Maurice reached the unmarked grave. Then he dug.

Four feet down, he encountered the concrete. Getting through it didn't take long, especially as imperfectly as it'd been re-laid. A hundred and twenty years later, nobody cared much about honoring the serial killer's final wishes. When the axes proved too slow, Maurice used his fists. They bled, but they healed. Maurice didn't care. All that mattered was getting this over with.

At the bottom of the rubble was what looked like an envelope made of rock. Maybe it was the first concrete they'd poured him into. Maybe it had partially collapsed. All he knew was that a moment later, he was starting at the remains of what used to be a human: an intact mustache on a skeleton's face, just like the internet promised. A skull full of teeth.

"I'm not going to do this," he said.

But of course, he did.

Into the grave.

With a pair of pliers from his back pocket, extracting the teeth.

Maurice climbed the side of the grave, then stood on the ground above it. An expression from a hundred bad-boy movies ("Roll dem bones") ran through his head. Then he tossed the teeth onto the ground like dice and spoke another phrase from the same book, now enshrined away from any world's fairs — but, thanks to the permanence of the internet, just a Google search away.

Maurice knelt on the ground, knees just south of where the teeth lay. He waited, feeling foolish, sure this wouldn't work. But there was another truism in his mind as well, and it was a logical treat: *After the impossible is eliminated, whatever remains — however improbable — must be true.*

And God knew, in 1893 he and his friends had eliminated all the impossibles. Holmes had still controlled them, even after the incantation. He'd still had a fist inside their heads, and there were only so many things that could do that.

Not a necromancer after all. Something else able to charm the undead.

The ground shook around the grave. It swelled upward, pushing against Maurice's bent legs. Maurice reached for the fourth tool then, and pressed it to the ground just below the teeth he'd spilled onto the grass.

Not the shovels.

Not the pickaxe.

Not the pliers.

But the blade.

The ground swelled in a man shape, long and lean, a head forming beneath the teeth. A few seconds later, he was kneeling on the chest of a man with teeth like a corpse's, now incorporated. According to legend, trapped.

But it was Holmes. Because that was the body he'd exhumed, because those were the teeth he'd pulled and offered for recollection:

Holmes.

He seemed surprised to wake with Maurice on his chest, holding him down, a massive edge against his neck.

"What the bother?" he said.

Maurice shifted, wanting to keep the man pinned. He wasn't sure if he was more happy that the incantation had worked or more terrified — for the present and the mistakes of the past.

Holmes looked up, his face somewhere between annoyed and pleased. And he said, *"Mr. Toussant?"*

"Did you really just say 'What the bother'?"

"Naturally. I'm British now."

"Should I get you a mirror?" Maurice asked.

Holmes seemed to understand. According to Maurice's research, the creature could only inhabit one body at a time. A long time ago, that body had been H. H. Holmes. Maurice had no idea which distant (and apparently British) body his bit of witchcraft had sucked the creature from, but being transported overseas to a forgotten gravesite with an angry vampire on his chest couldn't have been pleasant. It probably just wanted to go back — for Maurice to relinquish this bit of dark magic and allow the soul that had once been Holmes to fly back to re-inhabit his latest stolen body. Maurice, however, had no intention of letting that happen.

The man's hands went to his face. He felt that enormous walrus mustache and the soft face that, when it'd shuffled off the mortal coil, had only been 34 years old. His blue eyes were unchanged. Charm a man right out of his wallet, they could.

"Oh, fuck. I'm Holmes again, aren't I?" he said.

"Before they executed you, you said something I found interesting." Then Maurice quoted from Holmes's own confession: "'I was born with the devil in me. I could not help the fact that I was a murderer, no more than the poet can help the inspiration to sing. I was born with the Evil One standing as my sponsor beside the bed where I was ushered into the world, and he has been with me since.'"

"I was always so eloquent, no matter the body."

"But perhaps a bit grandiose," Maurice said. "Not the devil. A wendigo."

Holmes smirked. The blade bit the flesh of his neck. "How did you figure it out?"

"You had brotherhood with the dead. Ability to control the non-living, same as a human necromancer. Only ... the necromancer's refutation didn't work on you, did it?"

"I might have been any of a dozen evil things." It was surreal to hear him talk. Holmes had been American, through and through. The body Maurice reanimated was, by whatever laws these things had, more or less the same. Yet in the intervening years, the creature that had once inhabited H. H. Holmes had become used to the trick of a different accent. His Holmes voice was clipped and proper now and moved with a stiff upper lip, same as whichever hapless bastard he'd been living as until Maurice had called him home.

"Except that you were always hungry. Weren't you? You ate half of the people you killed. I wondered for years why you took Tatiana to the fair. It wasn't because she asked to go, was it?"

Holmes shrugged, still pinned. He made no effort to rise. Possibly because Maurice, who now knew what Holmes was and how to defend against wendigos, was no longer under his influence. Possibly because Maurice, for the first time in their acquaintance, had the clear upper hand.

"Tatiana wanted it to be her idea. I let her believe it was."

"You weren't after the book," Maurice said. "You were after the wendigo amulet that was in the same building."

"Can't bloody well possess a new body without it, now can I?"

Maurice shook his head, furious with himself for not piecing this together earlier. He wasn't to blame; he knew that much. Still, it was hard to forgive himself. Necromancers and wendigos could both protect themselves from vampires, but dealing with them took entirely different means. Necromancers had to be disarmed. Wendigos had to be counter-magicked. Both, once neutralized, could easily be killed.

All those people who'd died. All those people Maurice and the others had failed to protect.

"You're holding me down," Holmes said, "and yet you seem disappointed."

"I should have known."

"Face it, old chap," said Holmes. "I'm smarter than you."

Maurice pushed the blade against his skin. Holmes smiled. Now Maurice said, "*You* seem disappointed."

"Not at all. I've lived a hundred lives, but H. H. Holmes was the most interesting of them. You'll be pleased to know I turned over a new leaf after I left him, though. I was able to charm a guard into bringing me the amulet in prison as a 'last request,' then took his body. Nice man. I threw him off a bridge. I had another ready, of course, studied and prepared-for. That one lasted me twenty years give or take, then another, then another, and then my current host. All have been law-abiding, upright citizens. You have no qualms with me anymore, Maurice. Not for half a dozen lifetimes."

"I have many qualms with the one I knew."

"Come now," the wendigo said. "Have you no sense of forgiveness? I have children. I'm a doting father now. I run a small business and employ a staff of seven. I pay my taxes. Holmes is a distant memory."

"And when you need to eat?"

"Well," said the wendigo. "There is my true form for that."

"Show me."

"Are you sure? It is putrid. It smells, and is a poor conversationalist. If I become what I truly am, I might accidentally spear you with my antlers. I might cut you with my teeth. You might, out of disgust, kill me just to watch me die."

"Maybe I'll do that right now." He pressed the blade.

"Come now, Maurice. You are a good man. That is why you did not beat me a century ago. You were too trusting, as were your friends. Of course I knew what you were. Of course I knew your friend had turned the woman with all the tattoos. You were so concerned about not causing collateral damage that I slipped right through your fingers. You put your trust in law to punish the body that I'd taken. But what of it? I remained Holmes for as long as I could, and when I was done, I dismissed him. The body that hanged that day was barely a thing. They hanged dead meat, no more interesting than a side of beef. But that was then. This is now. You have changed. *I* have changed."

Maurice shook his head, wanting to swear. "I should have known. That fucking *blackout*. Necromancers can't cut off blood tie the way you did with Tatiana."

"Quite. But an impending possession? That will do it a treat."

"We stopped that much. We kept you out of Tatiana at least, you son of a bitch."

"Indeed. But how much was her life worth, anyway? Are you sure you did her a favor? Are you sure you did *anyone* a favor? I was done with murder already, you see. If you'd let me possess the tattooed lady that night, that would have been the end of it. Once I became the guard at Moyamensing, I was no longer a killer. Three years earlier, I might have stopped, had you allowed me her body to occupy." He tried on fake sympathy, his voice drawling. "But you had to have her, didn't you? And what price did Alice, Nellie, and Howard pay for your pride?"

Maurice pressed the blade, red rising behind his eyes.

"Judge me as you will," Holmes said, "but I did not kill Holmes's final victims. You did."

"Bullshit!"

"So angry. So goth! You are a parody of yourself, Mr. Vampire. You hate me for the lives I took — no more than a dozen, perhaps two. I forget how many, but in the end does it matter? *I* have since served over a hundred years of loving service to country and queen. In that same time, how many lives have you ended?"

"It's different."

"Is it?"

Maurice thought. The blade lifted, only slightly.

"Let me up, Maurice."

"You don't control me anymore."

"Exactly. Now the shoe is on the other foot. I promise you, Holmes is not who I am anymore. I haven't been Holmes for a long time. You are the murder now, Maurice. Not I."

The wendigo pushed, tempting the blade. It sat up using Holmes's body. Then, now side by side, it looked at him.

"You are far stronger than me. With my control lifted, I cannot make you do anything, or prevent you from doing whatever you wish. Go ahead, if you'd like. End me. But are you sure it's the right choice?"

It stood. Maurice let it.

"This body has already died. There is nothing you can do, nothing you can change. I am not a threat. On the contrary, I am a benefit to the world. The choice is yours." It spread its arms. "Come on now, Maurice. Prove to me that you are the creature I believe you are. Prove that you are incapable of forgiveness, of allowing change, of seeing the bigger picture. But hurry, will you? The corpse of Holmes is already returning to the earth. If you wish to kill me — to truly kill *me*, not just this sack of flesh and blood — use your blade and do it now."

Maurice watched. It was as if he was still paralyzed. Still under the spell. Despite his bleeding anger, he did nothing.

"You see?" said Holmes's body with a smile. "Even a vampire is capable of change."

Maurice looked down, at the dark soil of the Pennsylvania graveyard.

Then, in one rising motion, he swung the blade in a tremendous arc and separated the wendigo's head from its body. In the final moment, Maurice saw something on Holmes's face that he hadn't seen in life: shock. Despite knowing it all — despite the slippery, charismatic manner he'd once wielded like a weapon, H. H. Holmes had finally been surprised.

The body collapsed. It would, according to the ancient texts, disintegrate the way any normal corpse would. The grounds crew would arrive the next day to find the unmarked grave's dead man, dead all over again. The wendigo, however, was already gone for good.

As the body struck dirt and sloughed halfway into the concrete-lined hole, Holmes's head rolled to rest at Maurice's feet, that expression of shock still frozen on its visage.

Even a vampire is capable of change, the head seemed to repeat.

"That's what my therapist keeps telling me," Maurice told it.

ALSO BY JOHNNY B. TRUANT

Winter Break

Pattern Black

Pretty Killer

Cursed

The Bialy Pimps

Namaste

The Target

La Fleur de Blanc

Axis of Aaron

Devil May Care

Screenplay

The Island

Burnout

Sick and Wired

UNICORN WESTERN:

Unicorn Western

The Wanderers

A Fistful of Magic

Shimmer to Yuma

The Man Who Shot Alan Whitney

The Spectacular Seven

Open Meadows

The Unforgotten

The Magic Bunch

Unicorn Genesis

FAT VAMPIRE:

Fat Vampire

Fat Vampire 2: Tastes Like Chicken

Fat Vampire 3: All You Can Eat

Fat Vampire 4: Harder Better Fatter Stronger

Fat Vampire 5: Fatpocalypse

Fat Vampire 6: Survival of the Fattest

The Vampire Maurice

Anarchy and Blood

Vampires in the White City

Fangs and Fame

Game of Fangs

INVASION:

Invasion

Contact

Colonization

Annihilation

Judgment

Extinction

Resurrection

Save the City

Save the Girl

Save the World

Longshot

THE INEVITABLE:

Robot Proletariat

The Infinite Loop

The Hard Reset

Cascade Failure

Reboot

En3my

DEAD CITY:

Dead City

Dead Nation

Dead Planet

Dead Zero

Empty Nest

THE DREAM ENGINE:

The Dream Engine

The Nightmare Factory

The Ruby Room

The Pandora Core

The Engine Convergence

The Tinkerer's Mainspring

GORE POINT:

Gore Point 1

Gore Point 2

Gore Point 3

THE BEAM:

The Beam: Season One

The Beam: Season Two

The Beam: Season Three

The Beam Season Four

The Beam Season Five

Future Proof

Plugged

The Future of Sex

THE TOMORROW GENE:

The Tomorrow Gene

The Eden Experiment

The Tomorrow Clone

Null Identity

COMEDIES:

Everyone Gets Divorced

Greens

Fiends

Decoy Wallet

NONFICTION:

The Fiction Formula

Fiction Unboxed

Iterate & Optimize

The Story Solution

Write. Publish. Repeat.

The One With All the Writing Advice